Xenolith

the

Cynthia Pelman

Grosvenor House
Publishing Limited

Cover design by Tal Wagner

This book is published by
Grosvenor House Publishing Ltd
28-30 High Street, Guildford, Surrey, GU1 3EL.
www.grosvenorhousepublishing.co.uk

A CIP record for this book
is available from the British Library

ISBN 978-1-78148-470-8

Also by Cynthia Pelman

Joshy Finds his Voice

Voices from the Sand

This book is dedicated
to the memory of
Ignace Edelstein,
born 16th February 1903
and murdered in Auschwitz
14th July 1942.

Author's note

This book is based on my many years of working with children who have difficulty in finding their voice. Some of them have had challenges in developing speech and language; others have had general developmental delays. Some children were suffering from the effects of growing up in conditions of violence and deprivation. These are just a few of the reasons why children might struggle to find a voice of their own.

The child who tells her story in this book has a condition called selective mutism: she is able to speak, but not outside her home, or at school, or with anyone other than her own family. With the help of a speech therapist she learns to overcome her difficulties. This child and her family are fictitious; they are not based on any particular person or family, but are, in part, composite characters.

For more information on selective mutism please see the bibliography at the back of this book.

The other character in the book, Ignace Edelstein, was a real person, a victim of the Holocaust. I was allocated his name by the 'Guardian of the Memory' project, in order to honour his memory. I have tried to find as much information as I could about him and about his life; much of what I have written is speculative, but it is based on real facts.

A *xenolith* (Ancient Greek: "foreign rock") is a rock fragment which becomes enveloped in a larger rock. It is sometimes called an inclusion. It differs in origin and structure from the rock which encloses it. These rock fragments form at high temperatures and pressures, deep down in the mantle of the earth.

To be considered a true xenolith, the included rock must be identifiably different from the rock in which it is enveloped.

"And the too much of my speaking:
heaped up round the little
crystal dressed in the style of your silence."

From 'Below' by Paul Celan (1920-1970)

Contents

1

Stones

When I was five I started school, and I didn't speak for a whole year.

That is actually not totally accurate, and it is better to say things accurately if you say them at all. What happened was, I did speak at home, to my family, but I didn't speak to anyone outside the family. I didn't speak at school or anywhere outside the house.

Some people at school tried to get me to talk. Some of the teachers tried to be friendly, others got cross because I didn't talk, and some of them just gave up and walked away. And some didn't mind; it didn't bother them and they didn't bother me.

Actually, the first teacher I had, in Year One, was okay. She did her best not to let other people make me feel pressured. "Leave her alone, she's just a bit shy, she'll be fine!" she said.

Maybe I was shy, and maybe I wasn't. Maybe I am still shy, I don't know. But I didn't speak at school for the whole of my first year there.

Now I am thirteen and I do speak. But not to everybody, and not a lot. I still prefer to talk when I have something important to say. I don't like small talk, and I don't chat.

I do talk when I have to ask someone something, to get information. Getting information is what I do a lot of, because my interest is in finding things. Things that are buried, or lost. I look for buried treasure, for things that have to be dug up and uncovered. Or recovered. That is the career I have chosen for when I finish school: I am going to be a palaeontologist. Or a detective.

People in my family sometimes call me Am for short but my actual name is Amethyst. I don't mind being called Am, because it is who I 'am'. But I prefer to be called Amethyst by people who are not in my family.

At school someone once called me Amy for short. That was not okay. Amy is not my name; Amy is another name altogether. So even though I don't usually talk much, I did talk then. I told her my name is Amethyst, not Amy.

Since then nobody has called me Amy.

My father gave me the name Amethyst, because he is a geologist, and he chose names of stones or minerals for his children. My brother is Jasper. He is nearly nine years old. I am four and a half years older than him. My parents hoped they would have another child and they were going to call her Ruby, but that didn't happen.

I think my parents should have stone names too, like us. My mom's name is Carys but my dad sometimes calls my mom Crystal. It suits her. My dad told us it makes him think of crystal clear water when you are hot and sweaty in the desert. He spends a lot of time working in deserts so he should know.

We couldn't decide which name my dad should choose for himself; his name is Mike and that is not a stone name. But it is too complicated to change the name of a person who is already grown-up. He has his name on his driving licence and passport and his university certificates which prove that he is a geologist, so he can't really change it now.

It was from my dad that I learned what a xenolith is. A xenolith is the name geologists use for a rock which is embedded in another kind of rock. It is a completely different kind of rock even though they are joined together, one inside the other. At first glance it may look like part of the same rock, because it fits inside the rock, but it doesn't belong there and it doesn't really match.

And that is me. I am a xenolith, because even though at school I am one of the students, and I am part of my class, and these days I do speak to the other kids in my class and also to some teachers, I am a different kind of person and I am not really like them, and I don't really fit in.

I looked up the word xenolith online. In Ancient Greek, *xenos* means foreign, and *lithos* means stone, so I am like a foreign stone.

2

Words

Some people think that because I don't like to speak much, I don't like words. That is not true: I do like words, and I know lots of words. That is why I looked up the origin of the word 'xenolith.' I like to find out the origin of a word because it gives me a deeper knowledge of that word.

I am writing my own dictionary. My dictionary is not the same as any dictionary you might buy, where they just lump together any words as long as they are in alphabetical order, no matter if those words are interesting or not, or if they have anything in common with each other.

The only words I put in my own dictionary are words which I myself choose, and I only choose them if I like them, or if I need them to describe or to mark something important to me. I use lever-arch files for my dictionary, and that way I can add as many pages as I like because all you do is open the clip and put more pages in.

My dictionary is not in strictly alphabetical order. It is organized by topic. I group together words which have some similarity, either in their structure or their meaning. For example, I have a list of words which all start with the prefix 're'. In my dictionary they are listed under the heading *The World of 're'*. This is a group of words which describe what it is that I will do when I finally finish school (let it be soon) and start working in my chosen profession of palaeontology or detective work. The 're' words are:

> *retrieve, rescue, recover, restore, retain,*
> *remember, reclaim.*

These words describe what I am interested in doing: I want to spend my life searching for things that are hidden or lost. I sometimes think I am not interested in anything else.

Sometimes I enter words in my dictionary simply because I like the sound of them. Like the word *'thrive'* (see below). I also have a separate topic for Geology words, and a section titled Fossils, because I like collecting fossils and whenever I find a good one I look up its real name and write it down.

Even when I didn't speak to anyone outside our family, I used to collect words. I am not like some kids in my class who don't care how they speak and who use any old word to say things. They use verbs as if they were nouns; the other day someone in class said, "That is a big ask." And they use new slang words each week.

Words are important to me. I like to get them right and to know exactly what they mean. Even if maybe hardly anybody will ever hear me saying them.

The reason I like the word *'thrive'* is this: There was a writer by the name of Maya Angelou. She wrote books and poems and plays, and she died recently. She once said something important:

"It is important not merely to survive but to thrive. To thrive with some passion, compassion, humour and style."

That is why I like the word 'thrive'.

Maya Angelou was raped when she was seven and she didn't speak for years after that, but then she became a writer and a poet and she spoke up for Black people in America who were discriminated against. So not speaking doesn't mean you have nothing to say. Maya Angelou had plenty to say and she said it loud and clear. She said it when she was ready to.

I wasn't raped, nothing like that happened to me, but I also didn't speak for a while, and now I do.

3

Amethysts and other minerals

At the beginning of last school year, when I was twelve and a half, we moved house, to another city, and I had to change schools.

I had already transferred to High School when I was eleven, but the High School I went to before we moved was near my old Junior School, and so I started High School with all the kids I had known for years, and the change wasn't that bad. It is true that High School can be scary, because suddenly instead of having one class teacher who comes to your classroom, you have to carry your bag of books and go to each teacher's room; you have a different teacher for each subject and you go to a different room for every lesson. So that meant lots of change, and lots of complicated timetables, and lots of talk.

I think my parents were a bit nervous when I left Junior School; maybe they were worried that this kind of change would set me back a bit, with my history of selective mutism. Not that my parents talked much about that, and they certainly didn't call it that by name. The exact name for my problem is something I found out on my own, when I was about eleven and started to read online about speech therapy. When I asked my parents if that was what I had had, they looked a bit unsure of what to say, but they are scientists, and they like to be accurate and precise in what they say, so they said yes, and that my speech therapist, Mrs. Edelstein, who knew how to work with all kinds of speech and language problems, had helped me get over it.

So whatever it was then that made me silent, I was now officially not a selective mute person. Not any more.

But now, moving to a new city where I had no friends, and didn't know what the teachers would be like, was not a good change. And on my first day I made a bad start, because the geography teacher asked me a question and I hadn't been listening to what he was saying; I was planning a new topic for my dictionary, so instead of asking him to say it again, I just ignored him and stared at him and didn't say anything. I didn't actually mean to be rude, not then, on that first day, although since then I have developed a few rudeness strategies which I use quite often. But on that first day, he thought I was being rude, and he called me 'insolent' which I thought was rather a good word to put in my dictionary, along with some other 'in' and 'im' words:

*insolent, impertinent, insulting, impatient,
impossible, in-educable.*

He and I didn't get on from that day.

I had problems with other teachers at my new school too. I won't mention their names, but there were two teachers, in subjects which are quite important, and they started complaining about my not participating enough in class. They would call on me to answer questions, and sometimes, even though I knew the answer, I would get cross because I knew they were calling on me just to make me participate, so I pretended I didn't know. And they probably suspected that I did actually know the answer, so they were frustrated, and I was angry, and it wasn't going well.

The problems I was having with teachers reminded me of my first days in school, when I was five. I had never been to nursery or to playschool, in fact I had never been anywhere without my parents. My father's geology work meant he had to travel a lot, to many different countries, and when I was little my mother and I went with him wherever he went. So I never went to a child minder or to playgroup until that day, when I was five, and I had to start school.

Even though my parents had told me I would be going to school, and we had gone shopping together to buy a school uniform and a school bag and pencils, and they had driven past the school so I would know where it was, I didn't really know what was in store for me. I certainly didn't understand that once I had been there, on that first day, I would have to carry on going there forever. Day after day after day. And that our travels with my dad, going with him on his work trips, were now over.

I remember that very first day at school, even though it was eight years ago, when I was driven to school, and my parents suddenly drove off in their black car, my mother waving to me out of the window, and my new baby brother strapped in his car seat in the back, and they left me there. I didn't know what I had to do or why they had gone. Or when they would come back. Then a teacher came up to me and bent down low, and put her face next to my face and she spoke in a booming voice and she smiled so wide and looked at me so hard that I had to look down to get away from her eyes. So I suppose that's when it started, that's when I couldn't talk. I couldn't look at the teachers and I didn't want them to look at me.

After a while I suppose I got used to being at school, and I didn't feel so confused each morning, and I knew what I had to do each day, but I still didn't speak. My parents would drive me to school, and leave me there, and I had to sit through hours and hours of boredom until they came to fetch me, and in the meantime I didn't speak to anyone, and I would listen to the other children trying to learn their letters and sounds and I just couldn't understand why I had to be there. I already knew all the letters, in fact I could read when I was four, so it all seemed pretty weird.

My first class teacher in Year One thought I was just shy, so she left me pretty much alone and didn't try to make me talk. But she left shortly afterwards and we had someone new. This one was probably not cut out to be a teacher. Or maybe she just didn't know what to do with me.

I know what a real smile looks like. My mother has a real smile and though she sometimes looks in the mirror at the wrinkles at the side of her eyes and tries to smooth them out, I think her smile wrinkles are beautiful. Actually in our family we call them crinkles, not wrinkles, because they look a bit like crinkle paper.

But this teacher I am telling you about had neither wrinkles nor crinkles and I could see she was not happy with me for not talking when she wanted me to talk. She smiled at me with her lips but her teeth were clamped closed. Her teeth never smiled. And her eyes didn't smile either. She was not smiling all the way through.

But my name is Amethyst and I am named after a mineral and nobody can make me talk if I don't want to. A rock can contain different kinds of minerals, but a mineral is a mineral all the way through. I was stronger and harder than she was. So I didn't speak at school for the whole year.

And now that I am thirteen I do speak, but I prefer to speak only when I have something to say, and I prefer to say only what I mean. I speak when I need to, for example if I want to get information, or when I need to tell someone something important, and otherwise I don't say much.

4

Sand

Now that I think about it, I suppose it is not surprising that my geography teacher and I did not get on. He was a useless teacher because I knew more than he did. Once when he told us something, I put my hand up and told him that he was wrong. So it is not surprising that he hated me after that. But I couldn't just let it go; he was talking about deserts and that is my father's area of expertise and I knew he had made a mistake.

It is important to be accurate in science, and geography is a science, not a matter of opinion or style. So even though this teacher thought I knew nothing about geography because I don't ever do geography homework, I actually do know something about deserts.

The reason I know geography is because my father's work involves travelling all over the world, digging and exploring deserts and analysing sand. Sometimes when we went on a work trip with my dad we would stay in one place for months. When I started school I could have pointed out to you, on the globe which I still have in my room, every country we had been to, and I could tell you what language they spoke in each place, and what they liked to eat, and if that country had lots of rain or lots of drought. I knew which insects I was likely to meet and which animals might be dangerous, and I knew the names of the rivers and mountains in each place. So I probably knew more about geography and about languages when I was four than most kids know when they are my age now.

When I was small, before I started school, my mother and I would go with him wherever he went, and I had my own passport. I still have that original one even though it has expired. I keep it in a box in my room where I keep my important documents and papers.

If you look at that passport now you will see stamps from all over the world. We have been to lots of deserts: the Karoo in South Africa, and the Negev desert in Israel, and the Sonoran desert in Arizona. I remember the Panalu'u black beach in Hawaii, because I have never seen such black sand before or since. I remember the orange sand dunes in the Namib desert, bigger than buildings, with their sharp curved edges shaped like the wings of giant birds, and the black shadows cast by the dunes in the baking sun making curved lines which echoed the lines of the dunes, but not exactly; the shadow curves were somehow different, softer than the sand curves.

We used to go to all those countries because they have lots of sand and that is what my father studies for his work. He is an expert in sand. You may wonder what is so special about sand and why a person like my father, a clever person, could spend his whole life learning about and exploring sand.

My dad says that each tiny grain of sand can tell you a story, just like a book. And each story is completely different from any other story that sand can tell.

If you know how to read sand, what each sand grain is made of, and the size and the shape of the grains, you can find out about the geological history of a place. Sand travels around the world in ways people can't travel: it is pushed by wind or by ice or water, it moves huge distances across the earth and can tell us things about the world and how it was millions of years ago. My dad could tell you how each different type of sand moves and travels. Some sand grains roll, and some bounce, and knowing how sand travels or clumps or slides, he can advise farmers and miners and builders about the physical conditions in which they are working. My dad tracks sand like a hunter tracks an animal.

I learned about tracking when we were with my dad on his trip to the Kalahari desert. We had the help of a man who was from one of the hunter-gatherer tribes still living there. This man was an expert tracker and he showed my dad how to do basic animal tracking, and when he had some free time he showed me how to track people's footprints in the soft sand of the desert. Some things are obvious, like noticing in which direction the tracks are facing, but some are harder to read, like looking at the depth of the footprint to estimate how big or heavy the person was, if he was a child or a grown-up. You can tell if a person was walking or running, by the tracks their feet make in the soft sand. Even on grassy ground, you can tell which way a person was heading from the direction in which the grass was bent when a person walked over it.

I think I only started to really appreciate tracking when I got older and started to look for fossils, because I remembered what that tracker had told me: you need to know what you are looking for, keep a picture in your head, before you start to look. In a way, your eyes get sharper when you know precisely what to look for, and you will see more.

This is why words are important: giving something a name, a symbol, helps you to keep in mind a picture of the thing you are searching for.

The best tracking book ever written is by Louis Liebenberg, and he says this: even if you don't actually see the thing you are looking for, just knowing it has been there helps: your knowing helps you to think about where it would have been, what it would have looked like, and where you are most likely to find it. That kind of thinking gives you extra information that most people would not have. He says that you will be able to visualise the thing you are looking for, and – this is the bit I love best about what Liebenberg says – you will be able to create a whole story about the thing or animal you are searching for, "a story of what happened when no one was looking."

I have already told you that I am not like other kids; that I am a xenolith. I like to be alone, to think about new ideas, to learn new things on my own, using the internet or books, and I like to go on fossil-hunting trips. But I already saw, after a day or two at the new school, that at this school being a xenolith was not going to be okay. They needed me to fit in, to be like everyone else.

It's not like I started off at my new High School not speaking. I had changed since I was five. I now didn't have selective mutism, and the day before the move I decided that I would need to speak a lot at the new school, to be like everyone else, otherwise everyone would be on my case, and I would be the problem child again. But to tell the truth, when I saw how busy and big and unfamiliar the place was, with not a single person there that I had ever met, I knew it would be hard to speak there. So I suppose I was a bit quieter than usual, which for a person like me, who is normally quiet, means that I was quieter than anyone in the whole class, and sure enough the form tutor called me in after about a month for a 'chat'.

I sort of knew what was coming.

She was the English teacher as well as being my form tutor. She wasn't cross or anything, she just said she wanted to get to know me, because I was the only new kid at the school and she already knew all the others in my class. The other kids had been at the school since the previous year, or had at least started this year all at the same time, in September. I had started late, in October, a month after everyone else, so by then all the cliques had already been formed and I was the outsider, without even wanting to be.

She asked what I was interested in. So I told her a bit about geology, and archaeology, and fossils. And I suppose I was showing off a bit, because I wanted her to know that I am not stupid even if I am quiet, so I told her that I collect words and that I like to know the origin, the etymology, of words, and that I know things about the physical and chemical properties of sand and that I have visited deserts all over the world.

She asked me if I would write a special paper for homework. It wasn't the regular homework. The other kids had no choice; they had to write about a book we were reading in class, but she wanted me to write about myself, about what I was interested in, "So I can get to know you," she said.

So from then on, she and I had a kind of agreement. She knew I wasn't stupid, and I wasn't lazy, and she knew I preferred not to have to talk in class, but she did expect me to write something really serious each week. She was honest with me. She said, "I can't know if you are learning, because you don't like to participate in class discussions. And that's fine, I don't mind, but you need to give me something you have written so I know for sure you are learning."

I think this was a good agreement and I stuck to it. So this is the first piece I wrote for her, because she said I should write about what interests me.

5

The strategy of the search

This is the first paper I wrote for my English teacher:

Searching and discovering

By Amethyst Simons

I have three main interests:

1. *Fossils*
2. *Archaeology*
3. *Birds*

All of my interests have one thing in common: the things I like are to do with searching for things, finding things which have been hidden from view for a long time, or finding and naming new information about things which were previously unknown to me. I suppose you could say that my interest is in discovery.

Discovery does not happen by chance; you need to start off by doing lots of reading and by building your knowledge. You find the information first, and this guides you to know where to look, what clues to look for, and how to recognise something which may look to most people like a piece of broken rubbish, but which is actually a discovery. The knowledge you use for your search can come from different sources; in my case, it is usually from history, or natural history, or science.

Experience is also important, because when you start out on a search, if you don't have any experience, you may see something of value but not be able to recognise it.

It also helps to have the right technology to help you find things: in my case, it might be a magnifying glass, or a microscope, or binoculars. Or a camera.

Discovery gives you a feeling of excitement, of amazement even, and these feelings take over after you may have spent hours or weeks or months learning and preparing for the search. And when you do finally find a fossil, something you have been searching for, then just knowing you are retrieving something that was lost for maybe millions of years can take your breath away.

You can get the same feeling of amazement at a discovery when you look at something, say a piece of sandstone, first with your eyes, and then through a microscope. My microscope is a digital one which plugs into the USB port on my computer and when you look at different kinds of stones under the microscope you find clues to how the stones were formed and which minerals they contain.

My father, who is a geologist, showed me how he can slice a very thin section of a stone, in his laboratory, and when you look at it through his special electron microscope, you see all the crystals in the rock, glowing in different colours, as if a torch has lit them up. They remind me of stained glass windows.

If you don't have a digital microscope, you can use a cheap disposable camera and take out the lens. You stick the lens with blue-tack over the lens of your phone camera, and it will magnify an image. I have used this adapted camera while I am on a fossil-hunting trip to take pictures of fossils I have found, and I have been able to see all kinds of details which I couldn't see previously.

Archaeology interests me because it is about searching and discovering too. I like to watch the TV programme 'Time Team' because the team of archaeologists has got just one weekend to dig up a site and to find out as much as they can about who lived there, what they did and made, and what kind of buildings they lived in. Sometimes they find things like brooches or weapons or pottery kilns. They are always digging something up and it is often something amazing, that nobody really expected. Or perhaps there was something they hoped to find, based on their research, but were worried they would not find; they may search for hours and hours finding nothing, and suddenly – there it is.

You probably think that my third area of interest, birdwatching, has nothing to do with digging up treasure, but you would be wrong to think that.

Sometimes you see a bird you haven't seen before. You take the time and effort to look at it, to scrutinise it, in every detail. You memorise what it looks like: its main colours, how the colours vary on its head and neck and flight feathers. You watch carefully how it stands: its posture, its outline, its general shape and size compared to other birds. You try to see what it does when it flies: does it flap continuously, or does it flap and then glide? All these details help you identify it, and you go back to the bird books and look it up and you learn its name.

And then that name feels like a new treasure you have just discovered.

And even when you watch birds which are familiar, whose name you already know, and you watch them carefully for hours and hours, you can still discover something new about them, and that is like a new treasure that you have discovered too. You find out new things about how these birds behave, not just what they look like and their names. You might find out that this kind of bird moves around in flocks, and they always appear and leave in a group. Occasionally one is left behind on his own; he seems to notice it suddenly and flies off quickly to join the others, and you wonder if birds have personalities, and like to be different from each other sometimes, to be on their own for a while, even if they do belong to a flock.

Words are important, and the names of things are some of the most important words. By knowing that a bird has not just 'feathers' but flight feathers and contour feathers and down feathers, I can get to know each bird more completely: I can identify them more accurately and remember what each one looks like, because I know the name of the type of bird as well as the names of the parts of the birds.

Finding new facts about birds, by watching them for hours, is like the difference between listening to an orchestra on the radio, and going to see a live performance. When you watch a live performance, if you look carefully you can identify each instrument, when it comes in and what it sounds like, and then you have discovered something new, as new as if you discovered it in a secret cave or hidden in the clay at the bottom of a cliff.

All of these are ways to find something: to find buried treasure, to retrieve something that was lost or not known or seen before. You find it, you name it, and then you know it.

Part of the thrill in finding something lost is that once you find it and know it, it can't be lost any more. You can find out things that happened in the past, and the past doesn't have to be lost; it can be retrieved, recovered, and brought back to the present in some way.

I remember once, long ago, when we were on a trip to South Africa, I was sitting on the soft white beach sand at Seaforth beach, which is one of my two all-time favourite beaches in the whole world. I must have been about four because it was before I started school. I was digging idly in the soft, warm sand and suddenly there was something shiny; I had come upon four bright shiny fifty-pence coins.

I thought I had found a buried treasure. Later my parents told me it was just money that someone must have had in his pocket and which fell out while he was sitting on the beach. But for me it was my first find.

If I were asked why I have this interest, I would not be sure how to answer. It may be the search itself, and the challenge it presents me. It may be the thrill of the moment of finding something, when you suddenly see something; something that perhaps no human has ever seen. And certainly, there is a thrill in the reclaiming, the retrieving, of something that was lost.

But maybe the thrill is not in the finding, but in the knowing.

I actually enjoyed writing that paper for my form tutor. I usually like to call people by their names, just as I like to know the names of each fossil I discover and each bird that I watch, because names are important to me, but I won't say the name of this teacher because she asked me not to put her name in anything I write.

When I asked her why I shouldn't write her name in my paper, she said one day perhaps I will be a writer, and write a book, and she is a bit shy and she doesn't want everybody to know everything she said to her students in class, and to point to her and say "Oh, that is Mrs X, you know, Amethyst's teacher."

Well she was right about one thing, I am writing this book. But I can't see how she could be shy, because shyness is something I am an expert in. And the way she talks in front of the whole class, and the way I have heard her talking to other teachers at break, well, I don't think she could be a shy person.

Although you never know. Because as I have said, some things are hidden and need to be discovered, and maybe she has kept her shyness hidden because she wanted to be a teacher and you can't be a teacher if you are shy.

Anyway I will respect her wishes and I won't put her name in this book, but it is a pity, because she is a good teacher and she deserves to have her name written down somewhere.

Names are important. You have to treat them with respect.

6

The perfection of places

So that was how my English teacher and I made a bargain, and I stuck to my side of it. Each week I wrote a paper on a topic of my choice, and I gave it to her to mark. And don't think it was just for show, because she marked my papers quite strictly, and she made comments about style and about choice of vocabulary, and I had to revise some papers a few times before she was satisfied.

And it wasn't that she let me off the other work either: I had to write the same papers as the rest of the class, for English.

But she and I got on well and I actually enjoyed her classes and I felt I was learning a lot, and I stopped wishing I could be home-educated, at least in her classes. Perhaps she knew my history, maybe she knew that I had selective mutism when I was five, and perhaps she understood what it had been like. Or maybe she was just a good teacher.

The rest of my school life was not going well. I was spending most of my school day counting the hours and dreaming about our next holiday on the island: one of the most perfect places I have ever been to.

Nearly every year, for the summer school holidays, we, my mother and father and Jasper and I, go to a little island in the Aegean Sea which is in Greece. This summer holiday tradition started long ago, even before I was born, because my mom and dad liked to go there. He remembered it from when he was a child, and then it became a family tradition. We stay in the same house each year, which we rent for the whole holiday. Sometimes my grandmother comes with us, and sometimes other family or friends join us for a while.

It is a beautiful place. Above the town, the hills are still wild and covered in trees. The houses are mostly built lower down, near the sea and the port. Most of the houses are painted white, with blue shutters and doors. The climate on the island is quite dry most of the year, and besides the old pines, the one plant which seems to thrive there is bougainvillea. Most people have chosen a bright fuchsia-coloured bougainvillea. The plants creep up the sides of houses and over the gates and their pink and purple colour is so intense against the blue sky that you can't believe what you are seeing, especially when you have just arrived from a grey and dull England.

I like that colour fuchsia, and I love the word 'fuchsia' too. The name for the colour is derived from the name of the fuchsia plant, which was in turn named after a botanist called Fuchs who lived in Germany and published a book in 1542, in Latin. The book had accurate and detailed drawings of about 500 plants. That is one book I would love to have.

Of course the warm sun, and the clear turquoise sea, and the colours of the flowers and the blue sky are what make the island totally different from England and make it feel like a holiday place. But it is more than that. When we go there, my parents are relaxed, not working, and nobody has to rush anywhere or do anything at any specific time of day. One of us walks to the grocer across the road every morning to choose food for that day. Sometimes the neighbour who has a fishing boat brings us something he has caught for our lunch. Jasper and I can ride around on our bikes, because there are hardly any cars on the island, only horse-drawn carriages and motorbikes.

Early every morning, before it gets too hot, we go and swim, and the water is so warm and so clear, like pale green liquid glass, that you can see right down to the sea floor and watch little fish swimming about.

In the late afternoon, when it gets cooler, we ride our bikes or walk to the port, and my mom and dad meet their friends at one of the cafes next to the port. Jasper and I ride around the square on our bikes or have ice cream and watch the big yachts going in and out, and then we go and have dinner at one of the restaurants where you sit right on the beach, and the tide sometimes comes in and little warm waves splash on your feet while you are having your dinner. One restaurant has its own little flock of ducks which play around in the shallow water. Jasper and I always watch carefully, each year, to see if we can recognise them from last year, or if perhaps those ducks had been eaten for dinner one night and this is a new flock, but we can never be sure.

And of course there are the wild cats on the island, not really wild but feral, and sometimes they have the most beautiful little kittens who come down to the beach looking for scraps of food.

On the island, kids stay up late, and in the evenings even after it gets dark, the square in front of the big old hotel is lit up and all the kids hang out in groups, and sometimes I meet some people of my age and we stand near the sea and talk to each other and walk around till late.

Opposite our favourite beach on the island is a huge old school, which was once full of children but has now closed down. It is still sometimes used for conferences. Each year someone organises a 'Children's Olympics' in the sports grounds behind the school. The grounds are still looked after, and have lovely green grass and are surrounded by old pine trees. The fields are huge; much bigger than the sports fields we have in my school back in London.

The only sport in this Children's Olympics is running. Each age group has a race, even the little kids. Jasper's first race was when he was three and I thought he wouldn't know what a race was. But he got the hang of it: just run! And he ran half way around the field before the race even started and all the dads had to run after him to catch him and show him that you have to wait for the whistle to blow before you run. It was hilarious: all the mothers sitting up on the grandstand were in fits of laughter watching all those dads, some of them a bit fat and unfit, running after a little wiry boy.

Well, as you can imagine, I had always been a quiet person there. I did take part in the running sometimes but I didn't enjoy having everyone watching me. But that year, when Jasper ran and the dads ran after him, I had already finished going to speech therapy, and I didn't have selective mutism anymore, so I cheered as loud as any of the parents.

By that time I was seven and a half. My mother sometimes tells me the story when I ask her to remind me what happened to me. She says, you didn't speak at school at first, but by the time you were seven, you spoke in front of everyone, and you spoke whenever you needed to and whenever you wanted to.

That year I found a wonderful piece of fossilised coral, right there on the beach. I asked my father to help me look it up so I could label it properly, and we found out it is called a tabulate coral, and it is really beautiful because it has lots of little sections called corallites, which are polygon-shaped. My parents suggested that I should take it back to school after the holidays and do a show-and-tell on corals.

That was how much I had changed. I took part in the Children's Olympics, I helped organise the race for the younger kids, I cheered and gave instructions and took part in the race for my age group like everyone else. And after the holiday I did that show-and-tell in class without anyone helping me; I prepared a slide show, and I explained what corals are and how they can be living or fossilized, and I spoke in front of the class and had no fear.

My grandmother would sometimes come to stay with us at our house when my father went away for his work. It was always easy to speak to her, and she always knew what I would be interested in, and every time she came she had something special hidden in her pocket or her bag.

Once it was a tiny little box with a little lid, made of wood, and inside was a smaller box with its own lid, and inside that one, one even smaller. The whole thing could fit in the palm of my hand.

I think it was from that day that I started to love boxes, containers, places where you can hide and keep small things. I love boxes which have compartments, like tool boxes, and I love those antique wooden stationery boxes in which people used to keep their equipment for writing letters, when letters were still written by hand, before the age of computers or even typewriters. These stationery boxes often have inlaid wood decoration and little compartments for stamps and paper clips and envelopes. I think these are even better when they have a label on each section, saying what is inside each compartment. That way things don't get mixed up and don't get lost, and you always know where to find something.

I even love those Russian dolls made of painted wood, those matryoshka nesting dolls, which fit one inside the other, because even though they are not strictly speaking boxes, by which I mean they are not shaped like a cube or rectangle, they still contain things, in order of size, and when the one fits inside the next you know you have got them in their right order, each one fitting perfectly in its place.

So maybe when I talk about how I love boxes, what I really mean is, I like to be able to sort things into their places and categories, and to label them. But the box itself is also important: it has to be well-made, either of wood or high-quality plastic, and if it is made of wood, I like it to be wood which has been beautifully polished or decorated. It is what I call *The Perfection of Spaces*: each thing is in its own place and you know where to find things, and the container itself is as lovely as what is inside.

I have one box which I use to keep my collection of fossilized sharks' teeth. It is from Egypt, made of sandalwood, with a hinged lid. The box and the lid are inlaid with hundreds of tiny pieces of shell. The design is made up of perfect, tiny triangles, set in a pattern which is repeated over and over, and is called arabesque.

My uncle once bought an antique desk and at the back of the top drawer he found a false panel and in the little space behind it were some receipts that had been written when the desk was made, over a hundred years ago. They were the actual receipts for the making of the desk, signed by the carpenter who made it. I suppose the person who bought the desk put them there, maybe to remember how much he paid, or to remember the person who had made such a beautiful desk. Or perhaps the carpenter himself put them there.

It's not the false panel that I am interested in, because Anne Frank and her family had to hide behind a false panel in a wall, and that makes me feel sick, because of what happened to them in the end, and because of how it must feel to be suffocated behind a false panel. When I think of what happened to those people, I can't breathe.

It is the use of small containers to hide precious things, not people, that I am interested in. *The Perfection of Spaces* helps you to see more clearly, to find what you need to see. There is nothing confusing, nothing mixed up with anything else. Each thing is labeled and kept safe, perfectly in its place, and it can be found whenever you want to look at it.

But it is also about finding out something we didn't know, like finding out who made that antique desk, even though that person must have died over a hundred years ago. The receipt, signed with someone's actual name, put my uncle in touch with that carpenter; he could get to know him in some way.

When my dad told me about the desk and how my uncle found the hidden receipt, at first I wondered why anyone would want to hide a receipt. It isn't something that you would normally keep secret, and it isn't something particularly precious, in itself. But now I think I do understand what that person was doing when he or she hid it: perhaps it was the idea that one day, someone like my uncle, or even me, would find it and know who made the desk and how much it cost to make. It would be a way for that person, from years and years ago, to talk to someone living today. Things from the past can sometimes talk to you and you don't need words for that kind of talk, and you don't need to use your voice or have anyone listening to you talking aloud. It is a kind of silent message.

That is what I like about archaeology, and also about finding fossils which no human person has ever seen until you, the finder, dig them up: you can find things from long ago and recover them, and you receive a silent message that perhaps nobody else knows about.

Maybe it sounds to you like I am contradicting myself, because I said that I love to search for things which are hidden, and then I said that I like things to be organised and labelled and not hidden. But it is not a contradiction. I search for things so that I can find them, and once I find them I can know them, and I can keep them safe. But the search comes first.

7

A strategy of accuracy

The *Perfection of Spaces* isn't only about keeping things in their correct place; it is also about being accurate when you are talking about spaces and places, and when the geography teacher said things that were not accurate I spoke up and said so.

For once, I wasn't keeping quiet, even though the main complaint about me at the new school was that I was too quiet. So I was getting into all kinds of trouble at school; sometimes for speaking, and sometimes for not speaking.

'Sullen' is what one of the teachers called me when she spoke to me one day after a lesson. "You have an Attitude, you are Sullen, and it won't do you any good in this school my girl, so better snap out if it right now, and then we will get on just fine."

Well I didn't want to get on with her. I didn't like the way she taught and I didn't like her or her personality. Or her Attitude.

And the P.E. teacher also picked me out, in class, in front of everyone, for having a 'half-hearted attitude' and for having 'no team spirit' because I only like to do sports or activities which are solitary. Well that is true; what I like to do in P.E. is the fitness work. Fitness is something that is important to me, because if you are fit you can get out and go on long hikes to different fossil sites. It takes a lot of energy to keep going for hours, bending down, digging, and checking the tide is not coming in and that the cliff is not going to fall on you while you are digging.

In the school Mission Statement – I looked it up online – it says that they aim to give their students 'a balanced life', with academic fitness and physical fitness, and nowhere does it say that you can only get physically fit if you play team sports.

I am not a team player and never will be. I am not interested in belonging to a team and having us all win together, and I am not interested in getting a ball into a net or a goal or anywhere. I know I have to be fit to be healthy, but I can get fit by working out by myself in my room with weights, or by running on a beach, which I love doing. So why would I want to be part of the basketball team?

The thing I hate most about working in a team is that not everyone makes an effort. At school we are sometimes given projects to do in a small group. Usually it is left to me, because I hate it when people produce work that has mistakes or is half-finished, so in the end it always comes down to me taking it all home and fixing it up so that the presentation is correct, without mistakes, and looks good. So team work actually means, for me, that I have to do twice the work of everyone else. I suppose that is my fault, I asked for it, because I would rather turn in nothing than turn in something that isn't accurate.

If you do something it should be done well. Or not at all. And for some teachers, I choose not at all.

So I suppose I was the least favourite student of a whole bunch of teachers at my new High School. Well, that was something I could share with them: the feeling was mutual; we were the least favourite of each other. I certainly won't put their names in my book because that would make them famous and I am not going to help them be famous.

It was no surprise when the first parent-teacher meeting of the year ended with my parents coming home that evening looking serious and asking me to sit down with them to have a discussion.

I think that my dad was secretly a bit pleased with me when I told him the geography teacher had made mistakes and I had corrected him, but they didn't like it that I had no team spirit and that I was sullen and had an Attitude. And that I didn't do homework for certain teachers.

On the other hand my parents were not terribly upset because they had got such a glowing report from the English teacher about me and my work and my 'intellectual level' and my 'originality of thought' that it kind of offset the other complaints.

My mother said to me straight out, "Well, what do you think? Do you want to do anything about this? Or should we just leave it? Is it a big deal?" and my dad made some comments about getting a good track record in high school so I could go to a good university.

I have to tell you I felt very sullen in that conversation, and my Attitude was getting worse by the minute, because I hadn't wanted to change schools and I didn't like this new school or anything about it, but I knew he was right about university, so I tried to explain. I told them that I don't mean to be like that, I am just different from the others. I am not interested in the things most people in my class are interested in, and I am not a team player and I don't want to be. I just want to learn things that are interesting and to finish school as soon as I possibly can and go to university where I can study only the subjects I have chosen, and where nobody will care if I have team spirit or if I participate in group discussions.

But my parents being who they are, I wasn't going to get away with it, because they don't mind if I am not talkative or sociable but they do mind if I don't do well at school. They want me to be able to choose any profession I want to. They kept telling me I would have to meet the requirements of the Universities Admissions Service and get good grades to get into a good university. Seeing as I was only twelve at the time I really thought they were over-reacting; I still have years to go before I leave school. Unfortunately.

The next day my mother said she had an idea. What if they contacted Mrs. Edelstein, the speech therapist I used to go to when I had selective mutism, and asked if she could see me once a week and maybe she could help?

"Help me to what? I don't need her, I am not a selective mute any more."

"I am not sure really," said my mother, "but she knew you well, and I think you got on with her, so let's talk to her and ask her what she thinks we should do."

It turned out that since I had last seen Mrs. E. five or six years ago, she had done some extra studying herself, and she was now doing student counselling and coaching, as well as speech and language therapy. So that is how it happened that my parents arranged for me to go and see her once a week, for coaching.

I think they chose the word 'coaching' because they didn't know what else to call it, and they were worried that I would refuse to go if it was something like speech therapy, which I certainly didn't need any more. But when we talked about it, it didn't sound so stupid, because the plan was that she would help me with any homework I was stuck on (or refusing to do), but she would also see if she could help me to participate in class by showing me some techniques for confident public speaking.

To tell the truth I didn't mind going to see her. When I used to go and see her once a week, when I was still a selective mute, I had enjoyed our time together. And I thought, if it gets those teachers off my back I will agree to go and see her once a week.

And even though I had last seen her years ago, I remembered that she had never forced me to do anything I didn't want to; she never once tried to make me talk when I wasn't ready to, and she didn't stare at me. She didn't think I was stupid. She would explain why we were doing whatever it was we did in speech therapy, and how it would help me not to be so scared of speaking, so that I understood why I was there.

So that's how I started to go to Mrs. E. again, once a week, just as I used to go to her when I was five and I had selective mutism.

8

Meeting Mrs. Edelstein

When I first started going to speech therapy with Mrs. Edelstein at the age of five, a few months after I started school, it wasn't because I couldn't speak; I just didn't want to. Well, not at school or outside the house.

At home I spoke to my father and mother, and I spoke to my grandmother. But because I was not speaking at school, or when I went with my mother to the shops, or in the park when other people were there, everyone got worried.

Anyway, it was to my grandmother that my parents turned for advice, all those years ago, when the school told them I wasn't speaking, because she knew me so well. I know they asked her for advice, because I overheard them talking to her on the phone one evening. By then I must have been at school for about three months.

When they had that conversation, they thought I was sleeping but I was awake, sitting on my favourite step in our old house, the one we lived in before we moved. There was a special step, just where the staircase from the ground floor to the first floor turned a corner, and nobody could see you if they were downstairs, but you could hear everything the grownups were saying.

I used to like sitting on that step sometimes when I had to think about something, or even when I just wanted to read but didn't feel like being in my room. Most people knew that if they were looking for me they might find me on that step; when I was little, if I wanted them to see me I would go down a few steps, but if I wanted to hide I would go back up to my special step. Sometimes my parents had visitors who stayed for hours, and they had no idea that I was sitting up there, listening to them, because they couldn't see me if I chose not to let them see me.

So that evening, when I was five, when they phoned my grandmother, I could hear they were upset, but I couldn't understand why they should be upset, because my parents knew I could talk, and my grandmother knew I could talk, and so did I. It's just that at school I didn't talk, and only the teachers were upset and why should my parents care about that?

And even though I knew people were worried, I didn't see that there was anything to be done about it. But my parents wanted to do something about it, so they decided to send me to a speech therapist.

The first time I met Mrs. E. I remember that my parents didn't tell me she was a speech therapist; they called her a teacher, but on her wall outside her house there was a sign saying 'Speech and Language Therapy' so I knew what I was there for.

Lots of people thought that because I didn't speak I couldn't read, but when I started to go to the speech therapist I had been reading for a whole year already.

I could read before I was five, because my mother taught me.

I remember that I wasn't happy when I saw the sign saying 'Speech and Language Therapy' because I was worried that she would try to make me speak. But she didn't. After saying hello, she hardly even looked at me. She just opened her toy cupboard and it was packed with games. I had never seen so many games outside a toyshop. She said I could choose any game I wanted but I didn't know what to choose so I didn't choose anything.

Then she took out some coloured markers and paper and asked if I wanted to draw, but I didn't want to draw.

I remember how quiet her house was, and I remember a very specific clear, sharp, sweet smell. I found out years later that she used candles with a fragrance which I still love: wild honeysuckle. You can buy them at the shop at Kew Gardens.

I remember she took down, from the top shelf, a big flat plastic box, with a handle. It was the kind of tool box you can get in hardware shops. I knew those boxes because my dad sometimes kept his stone samples in them. The boxes are divided into lots of small sections so you can keep each thing separate.

These days I have several of those boxes, and I keep my fossils in them. I like to keep them separate, so they don't get mixed up, and each one is in its own space. I write little labels which say what kind of creature or plant it was, and I also write down where I found it and what the date was when I found it.

Most people prefer to note the date when the fossil lived – or rather the period: like Jurassic, or Devonian. But these time periods which lasted millions of years are not something I can relate to. Numbers that big are not something I can visualise or imagine. So I prefer to write the date on which I found the fossil, because that way I can show that I respect the thing it was before it died: it is in a way like a tombstone, with a name and a date on it. This is an example of *The World of 're'*: I rescue the fossil and remember when I found it.

Anyway, when I saw that Mrs. E. had the same kind of toolbox my dad had, I kind of relaxed and stopped worrying. The way she had arranged her box was that each compartment contained a different miniature toy. There was a tiny porcelain egg, a model car, a beautiful wooden chair. There were little people, and little animals and even little monsters. All the toys were beautiful, and interesting, and there were so many different things to look at. So I picked one up and held it and then I put it back.

She took out an empty box, just a plain cardboard box with a good lid, and said, "This one will be for you. We can write your name on it. Every time you come here, you can choose from the toys in this big tool box, the ones you really like, and keep them in your box. Your box stays here with me, you can't take it home, but it will be here for you to play with each time you come and see me."

So I chose a few of the miniatures which I really liked, and I put them in my box, and she took a sticky label and stuck it on the box and I wrote my name on it, and she showed me where she would keep it, in a special cupboard, so it would be safe until I came again. She said that I would always know where to find it, because it would always be in the same place, and nobody else except me could open it, and nobody except me would be allowed to play with those toys.

Then the session was finished and we went home.

9

The strategy of small steps

When I was still a selective mute I went to the speech therapist once a week, every week, for a really long time. It must have been for more than a year, because when I started going, I was five, and I remember it was winter, and I was still going to her after the summer holidays, after I had turned six. And the next winter, when it snowed, and she left her kitchen window open by mistake and the snow was all over her floor, was when I stopped going to her.

I remember something beautiful from my visits to Mrs. E. in those days. She had an unusual kind of doll's house, which didn't look anything like a typical English house with a pitched roof. It was a very special kind of house: a tree house.

And when I say 'tree house' I don't mean a little house inside a tree; I mean that the house itself was a tree. It was made of branches and logs and it looked like a fantasy house for gnomes living in a forest. Each floor of the house was made of a slice of wood, lying horizontally, with its bark still around the edges, and instead of walls holding the next floor up, it had little logs, and little branches, with the bark still on them, and they held up each floor. There were wooden steps and rope ladders made of sticks and string, leading from one floor to the next, and right at the top was a wooden balcony perched on top of a branch: a lookout post, with rope around it so people wouldn't fall off.

Even the furniture was made of logs: a small log with a niche carved into it made a bed; two little bits of a branch were stuck together to make chairs or sofas; the little tables were made up of circular slices of logs, with a central leg made of a tiny twig.

Mrs. E. had attached three little doorbells, wired up to tiny batteries, so that the house had a different doorbell at each level. At first, when she showed me where to press the button to ring the doorbells, I was entranced. Real doorbells on a doll's house! But it took me a while before I felt ready to ring the bells on my own because they were quite loud, and when they rang I thought people might hear it and come and see who was ringing and then I would be expected to talk. In those days I not only didn't talk, I didn't make a sound if I could help it.

In those days I hated people looking at me. Being looked at was almost as bad as being expected to talk, and by being very silent and still I could make sure nobody would even know I was there.

But there was nobody there to look at me except the dolls, and Mrs. E. of course, who didn't ever stare at me or try to make eye contact, which some teachers thought was so important. So one day, very slowly, I reached out one finger and gingerly touched the bell without ringing it, and then I touched it softly again, and again, and then I took a big breath and I pressed the button and I rang the bell.

It was quite loud. I felt alarmed and looked quickly at Mrs. E., but she didn't seem to notice; she was having a sip of water, and my mother was in the other room reading, and so I rang that doorbell again, and listened to that one, and then I tried the other two, with their different rings, and somehow it felt alright, making a bit of noise in that room. I guess that would have been considered progress, even though I was still not speaking at all outside our own house.

One day, Mrs. E. asked me if I would mind if my mother came into the room to see how I had arranged the dolls and the furniture in the tree house, and of course I agreed (not by speaking but by nodding 'yes') because I didn't mind talking in front of my mother. When my mother came in to the room, Mrs. E. tactfully went out of the room to get us all a glass of water, and in the meantime I was showing my mother everything: the doorbells, and the furniture, and the lookout post, and explaining why I had arranged things the way I did, and which doll lived on which level, and which doll rang which doorbell, and when Mrs. E. walked in with the water, I just carried on talking, for a few words anyway, until I realized she was listening.

And what I really liked about Mrs. E. was that when I did finally talk in front of her, she somehow showed me she was pleased, but in a quiet way: she didn't make a fuss, there was no loud cheering or 'well done' or 'good work' like some teachers do, and thank goodness for that, because if my talking had led to her making a big excited bother I would have stopped talking instantly.

I remember playing with that tree house week after week. I would make up a family who lived in the tree house and sometimes the people in the tree house spoke to each other and I would sometimes let Mrs. E. hear what they were saying to each other. It wasn't really me speaking; it was the family in the tree house. At least that is how it felt to me at the time.

And that is how Mrs. E. helped me to talk in front of her, because before that I had felt very happy going to play with her each week but I didn't speak and only nodded or pointed when I wanted something. But from those times when my mother came into the room and Mrs. E. was going in and out quietly, getting water or tea or tissues, I started to speak, first in front of her and then, actually, to her.

Now that I am thirteen I can see how she did it. She had a *strategy*, just like my brother Jasper. He wants to be a magician when he grows up, but he will never tell us how he does his magic tricks; all he will say is "I have a strategy." Mrs. E.'s strategy to help me to talk without fear was a *Strategy of Small Steps*.

She would tell me that she knew it was sometimes hard for me to talk, but that there were things that could help, and coming to speech therapy was one of those things that helped. She talked a lot about 'next steps', and she often told me that we would only take tiny steps; we could stay on the same step for a long time, for as long as I wanted to, and we would only change one tiny thing each time, and if that was too much we could go back to the previous step.

And she said, over and over, that I would be the one to choose whether to take a next step or to wait a while on the same step. So she would never force me to do anything, and she always made me feel safe, like I was in control in some way.

I knew what she meant about steps, because I used to spend so much time on the steps of our old house, especially on my special step, just where the staircase turned a corner and people downstairs couldn't see me.

When I think about it now, now that I am not a selective mute person any more, I think her strategy of small steps worked because it allowed me to get over my fears very, very slowly.

There were two main things we worked on, and she described them to me as if they were two separate staircases to climb. The first staircase was about people and the other one was about places.

The *'people staircase'* was about slowly adding to the number of people who would hear me speak. So I started off speaking only to my parents and my grandmother; then I spoke to Mrs. E. alone in the room, and then, after a really long time, I started to speak to one or two other carefully-chosen people. The aim was to help me to eventually be able to speak in front of anyone who happened to be there, and in front of the whole class.

The *'places staircase'* meant that I had to get used to talking in many different places, and not just at home. So in therapy I first learned to speak to Mrs. E. in her office, and then I had to extend it to other places: outside her room (for example in her kitchen) and later outside her house, and eventually in the playground, and finally in the classroom. One step at a time, one staircase at a time.

I sometimes think about that time. To this day I don't know why it happened, why I didn't speak. But I do know that there isn't an easy answer, and it wasn't one thing that set it off. It's not like I had a trauma, or a bad childhood, or a life like Maya Angelou. I had a very nice life and I still have a nice life. But even now, now that I can talk at school, I still don't really like to chat, and I don't do small talk. It is just not me.

But what I do know is that Mrs. E.'s *Strategy of Small Steps* did help me get rid of my selective mutism.

Don't think it is a magic cure. Don't think that after I finished going to speech therapy I never felt the pull of silence.

And now I was back with Mrs. E. after all those years. Her house looked the same and I immediately noticed the same sharp, sweet wild honeysuckle smell. She had placed the perfumed candle on the windowsill, in exactly the same place she used to put it when I was little.

And there was something else which was entrancing, and I don't know why I hadn't remembered it from my visits to Mrs. E. all those years ago, because I recognised it immediately: she had a stained glass window panel in her front door, and when you walked into the house there were colours all over the wooden entrance hall floor. It felt like you could step into the pools of coloured light and disappear there if you wanted to.

What she said to me this time was, "I don't know if I can help, I don't even know if there is any problem to be solved here, but do you want to give it a go and see if we can find out together?"

To give her credit, Mrs. E. never said she knew something if she didn't. She had this thing she would do, a mannerism which I always associate with her: she would put her hand to her chin and tilt her head to the side and look up, and she would say 'I wonder…' and suggest that we try to find out together whatever it was she was wondering about.

10

Fossils

This is the second essay I wrote for my English teacher after we came to that agreement.

<u>Getting your eye in</u>

<u>By Amethyst Simons</u>

People often ask me why I love searching for fossils. They are worried about all kinds of things – cliff falls (this does happen in England, quite often) and falling on the rocks (that can happen too; my mom once broke an ankle when she slipped on a rock while searching for fossils in Folkestone) and high tides coming in.

But it is not just the risks that people are concerned with. It is rather that they just don't see the attraction of reaching under slimy, seaweed-covered rocks for little dark broken pieces of stone in the hope that you will find the remains of something which lived millions and millions of years ago.

Some people ask me why I don't just go to those shops which sell fossils, fossils which have been prepared and cleaned and polished, and buy the best examples of each type that I can afford.

And my answer is, it is not the having of it, but the finding of it that matters.

It is the thrill of the search; it is getting to that state where your eyes see more sharply than usual, where your vision is super-charged, like an eagle. It is being a detective. It is that moment of discovery.

When you start out on any particular day, it takes a while to 'get your eye in'. At first you find nothing. You are reaching under rocks, and you keep thinking that if you just move a few inches to the left or the right, or just under that rock over there, that is where you will find something. You know you only have forty-five minutes before the tide comes in.

If you are feeling brave you dig a little in the clay at the base of the cliff, although it is safer to stand as far from the cliffs as you can, especially after a rainy winter, when the cliff is undermined by water that has seeped in from the top and a rock fall can happen at any time.

You are bent almost double, your back starting to ache from the backpack you are carrying. The backpack gets heavier and heavier as the time goes by because you are picking up rocks which look like they might have something interesting inside them, but you don't stop to try to break them open with your hammer because you are working against time. So you also pick up broken bits of not-very-special fossils because maybe you won't find anything better on that day, or maybe you don't have time to examine it right then with your magnifying lens but it looks kind of interesting; and it all goes into the bag on your back. And you are also carrying water and food and Ziploc plastic bags, and a rain jacket and a hat and sunscreen and spare shoes, because sometimes the clay sticks to your shoes and you can't get back onto the train with sticky filthy shoes.

But then – suddenly – after wishing and hoping and visualising what you hope to find, you see something. You see a pattern, a regularity, maybe a vague hint of a spiral, or some lines which look too regular, too parallel, to be just a broken flint. It may be tiny, a little ammonite, but perfectly formed, and suddenly, like a flash, you see it, you reach for it, you feel it, you have it.

It makes you stop breathing for a moment. It is a revelation, and you feel a rush of wonder. You are the first – no, you are the only human, ever to have seen and touched the remains of this little creature.

And it is you who searched for it, you who didn't give up, you who found it.

You wrap it up carefully in tissue paper and put it in a Ziploc bag so it doesn't get lost among all the other debris you have picked up. And after that you can climb back up to the walkway, eat some of the cheese you always carry with you to give you energy, and go to the public loo to rinse your hands and your finds, and start the long journey back home.

A fossil is often not even an actual creature, and it is often not even the skeleton of the creature. Sometimes what you find is some minerals which have seeped into the shell of what was once a creature and created a shape which now simply resembles the original. It might be just the imprint of a wave which moved across some sand, creating curved lines, now solidly imprinted in stone. Or you may find just the tracks left by the feet and tail of a trilobite who walked on soft sand, tracks which got preserved because some more soft sand fell on them and buried and preserved them.

But seeing that shape, or that stone, finding it and taking it home, means that in some way you have kept it alive even though the creature who moved there, who left his tracks or died there, was on this earth millions and millions of years ago.

In a way it is like bringing something back from the dead.

Everybody who knows me knows I love fossils. My favourite place to look is among the rocks on Folkestone beach, because we nearly always find something there. But you have to plan very carefully because the tide comes in quite fast, and if you are a long way out you may not get back to the walkway in time. We are very careful to check the tide tables each time we go, and we keep checking our watches while we are on the beach so we won't make a mistake.

Once, after we had finished searching, and had climbed up the rocks to the walkway above the beach and gone to the nearest cafe to have a cold drink, I looked back at the beach where we had been walking. The sea had covered the beach completely, and had come almost three quarters of the way up the cliff, as high as a multi-storey building. If we had stayed on the beach we would have been covered up completely, along with the fossils and the dinosaur footprints and the rocks and the seaweed. So you have to know how to plan carefully when you go looking for fossils, otherwise you could end up a fossil yourself.

We have a family tradition for birthdays. We don't get birthday presents or have big parties; instead the person having a birthday gets to choose to go travelling somewhere. My mom doesn't mind parties, and Jasper will agree to go to a party if they ask him to do a magician show for the kids, but nobody else in the family likes parties. If someone offered my dad a choice of how to celebrate his birthday he would choose a trip to some desert to look at sand; he would definitely refuse to have a party.

Of course birthdays don't always fall during school holidays so the actual birthday trip is often months after the birthday itself. So what my mom does, for the actual birthday, is make a giant birthday card. Some of them are really huge, as long as your arm. She cuts out of magazines or travel brochures pictures of the place the birthday person has chosen to go to, and the person whose birthday it is has to do some research and make a list of what he or she wants to see and do there, and my mom sticks the pictures and the list into the card.

If she can book tickets for any special shows or museums in the place we are going to, she makes a cardboard pocket which she sticks inside the birthday card and places the tickets in there. She sometimes collects some of the money they use in that place, and puts it in transparent little coin holders, all stuck into the birthday card. And she cuts out something written in the language of that country and pastes it in: maybe a few useful phrases like 'I am a vegetarian' or 'where can we catch a bus to the beach.' So you can see how it can take months to make the card.

I suppose that is why Jasper and I know so much about other countries, about their language and culture and even their money, and what people do in those places. Jasper never did as much travelling as I did, because when he was born I was already in school and we weren't travelling much except during the holidays, but if you add up all the birthdays our family has had, it means he and I have been to lots of different places.

For my thirteenth birthday I chose to go on a fossil-hunting holiday. My birthday is in April, so during the Easter break we went to Folkestone for four days to look for fossils.

Everyone in my class who is turning thirteen this year has a big party, with music and special lights; it is what everyone is doing. But I didn't want a party, I wanted a fossil trip, and one or two girls in my class made some rude comments about me, because they thought I was weird not having a party and preferring to go to the beach when it wasn't even summer. A few of them don't invite me to their parties, which is no problem for me because I don't want to go anyway.

So you can already see that I am a bit different from other people, or at least other people of my age. Maybe that is what those teachers didn't like about me.

In a way I was glad the teachers complained about me because it ended up with my going to see Mrs. E. again.

It's not that I wanted to learn how to fit in with the other kids in my class. I was definitely not interested in that. But I agreed to go and see her because she is interesting, and also because I knew that then my mom and dad would stop worrying so much about me. I hate it when they worry about me and talk about me in that strained anxious voice they both have.

I suppose I should describe what kind of person Mrs. E. is so you can picture her. When I was little and used to go to her every week because I didn't speak, I already knew she was different from any other teacher, because she didn't try to make me speak, or to make me do anything, for that matter, that I didn't want to do.

She didn't talk loudly, and she didn't smile huge smiles. And she didn't stare at me. If I didn't want her to look at me or to hear me speak she would never force me, and if I didn't feel like playing her games I could choose something else.

I think one of the best things about her was that she knew how to be silent, how to sit with me and not feel that she, or I, or anyone, had to be talking all the time. And she always explained her strategies to me, her small steps, so I was never surprised by anything that happened.

And now that I know her in a different way, now that I am thirteen, she is still different from any other teacher, because if I don't feel like doing the work she sets me on any particular day she is happy if we just sit and chat.

When I think of her now, I suppose because I am a lot older and I know things I didn't know then, I can see other ways that she is different from other teachers. Teachers usually know a lot, or at least they want us to think they know a lot, but Mrs. E. often doesn't know things. Like Twitter and Instagram: she knows nothing about that, though I wouldn't really expect her to, because she is quite old. She is a lot older than any of my school teachers.

I know exactly how old she is, by the way, because not long ago when I went to her house there were birthday cards on the table in the entrance hall, and one of them had a big '63' in glitter on the front. So she is a lot older than my parents and I think she is older than all my school teachers too. In fact I don't know anyone else as old as she is except for my grandmother, who is 68.

I think I am getting old myself, because I am trying to write about Mrs. E. and what kind of person she is, and I keep getting sidetracked. Let me try to describe what she looks like.

She has grey hair, which even my grandmother doesn't have. My gran does not have grey hair because she goes to the hairdresser every month and has her roots touched up. Mrs. E.'s hair is grey and shortish, and smooth, and she has a floppy fringe which gets in her eyes so she has to brush it to the side all the time.

She wears glasses. She must have about five different pairs, and that's another thing about her: she keeps losing them and finding another pair so you never know which one she will be wearing. She keeps taking them off and putting them on; sometimes she uses them on top of her head to hold her floppy fringe back, and then she will leave them on top of her head and start looking for her glasses. Once she was wearing two pairs of glasses at the same time: she had one on her nose and another pair on top of her head, and for a while she didn't notice.

Maybe it's because she is old that she forgets not just where she put things, but also what we are meant to be doing in our sessions. When I went back to see her, after the teachers complained to my parents, she wrote down some targets for our work together, like working on public speaking and confidence, and 'managing conversational flow' (that was her idea of course) but I usually manage to get her sidetracked by other things so we often don't work on our targets at all.

Or maybe she is just very sharp, because I have noticed that even when we are not working on our targets, but just talking about all kinds of things, just chatting really, and she is being curious and wondering about things and saying 'Hmm...' a lot, she is looking at me out of the corner of her eye. And maybe she thinks I don't notice, but every conversation we have ends up with me talking and talking, and telling her ideas I didn't even know I had until we got into that conversation. Considering that I am accused of being a non-participator in class, I seem to be able to talk a lot, and I sometimes surprise myself how much I talk when I am in Mrs. E.'s office.

11

Dreams of flying

In my first session with Mrs. E. after my mother arranged for me to see her to keep the teachers happy, she asked me what was going on at school, and why I had come to see her.

I told her it wasn't my idea, but then I thought that sounded rude, because she would think I didn't want to be there, and actually I didn't mind going to see her. At least it got my parents off my back. So I told her about the teachers who were complaining about me, about my Attitude and that I was sullen and I didn't participate and didn't have team spirit.

She asked if it was only the teachers complaining, and I told her that my mom and dad weren't exactly complaining but they were looking at me in that worried way they have which I hate.

Actually I was furious that my parents were worried I wouldn't do well at school and I wouldn't get high enough marks to go to a good university, because I know I can do it and I don't believe you have to do homework to get good marks in the final exams, and I thought they would have known I am capable of doing well. I was starting to wonder if they too had doubts about my ability.

I didn't know how to explain it to Mrs. E. so she would know how stupid this whole thing was, how it had been blown up into a big problem, when actually there wasn't a problem because school is supposed to be where you learn certain things and pass your exams, and I was doing all of that.

I knew that the whole fuss was actually about what teachers expect you to be: just like everyone else. And I was not going to try to be like all those kids, who speak in half-sentences and pretend to be oh-so-sociable in class, always answering the teacher's questions in just the way that makes a teacher happy, but in the meantime they spend all their hours outside school with their heads bent over their phones, texting, tweeting, and not talking to anyone. And definitely not talking to me, the class weirdo.

My silence, the fact that I don't talk much to other people, is actually no different from theirs in quantity, but very different in quality. Mine is a silence which is thought-out, a silence by preference. Theirs is just because they are too busy texting to talk.

But Mrs. E. was not interested in the other kids. She wanted to know more about the main complaint against me, about not participating.

"So some of your teachers complained to your parents that you don't participate in class. Can you tell me a bit about this participation, so I know what it is?"

I told her it is the kind of behaviour you have to show in the classroom: putting your hand up and saying things when the teacher asks you to, but not speaking when the teacher doesn't want anyone to talk, even if you have a good point to make. The teachers are always asking questions in class, and the kids who are good participators always put their hands up and have something to say to answer a question. I think participation is more about pleasing the teacher, complying with what the teacher wants, than about learning or thinking about new ideas.

"And is it that you don't put your hand up, you don't participate, because you don't have an answer to those questions the teachers ask?"

"Of course I do! I know exactly what the teachers are asking! I just think it is stupid to answer because the teacher doesn't want us to really have a conversation, she just wants us to say what is already in her own head so that she can get on with the lesson."

"So these teachers, they ask a question and they already know the answer?"

"Usually. I sometimes think, why don't they just set us a test, then we can all write down our answers to the questions, and it will be over, and nobody will have to talk, and even better, nobody will have to listen to other kids saying the same thing over and over. It is completely boring, and if that's what they want me to participate in, well I am not going to."

By this time I was furious, just thinking about the whole thing and the fuss everyone was making about nothing.

"Hmm… I wonder…" said Mrs. E., her head tilted to the side, looking up at the ceiling.

It is a good thing that Mrs. E. likes to take a few minutes to think, to be quiet, because it gave me a few minutes to calm down. I was so irritated by this whole stupid panic about the teachers' stupid complaints that I couldn't think straight.

Mrs. E. finished thinking and wanted to know more. "So am I right," says Mrs. E., "that participating means having boring talk, saying things over and over, and listening to people saying what was already said?"

To be completely honest, there was more to it than that, though she had got it partly right. The thing is, that when the other kids say something, maybe I know more about the subject than they do (this happens in geography especially) or they are using exactly the same words the teacher used and they haven't even thought how you can use words to say things which are nearly the same, but not exactly the same, and in the end I can't stand it that they see it so narrowly, and that they speak so quickly, without taking time to think, and I have so much I could say ... but I kind of freeze; I don't think they will get it anyway if I tell them my ideas, and I am sure the teachers would hate it if I was always Miss Know-it-all.

Like that time when I corrected the geography teacher; he has never forgiven me for that. I know he hates me and it is completely mutual.

I told Mrs. E. that just sitting there in class, listening to questions and answers, questions and answers – that is what makes me wish I was somewhere else, maybe on the beach in Folkestone looking for fossils, or swimming in the sea around our Greek island. And that is when the teachers see that I am dreaming and not listening and that is when they call on me and I don't know what they have been talking about and I just stare at them. And that is when they talk about my Sullen Attitude.

Mrs. E. couldn't leave it alone. She asked me what I thought the teachers would want me to be doing, if I *was* actually 'participating.'

"Those kids who do participate, what do they actually do in class so that the teacher knows they are participating? I don't mean what they say, but what do they *do*?"

"They put their hands up, they give the right answers to the teacher's questions."

"And you...?"

"I know the answers, and I don't put my hand up. I don't see why I have to tell the teachers what they already know. If I fail an exam, if I write rubbish papers, then I can see that they have something to complain about."

"So," said Mrs. E., "You are sitting quietly, and this quietness, this silence of yours, is causing people to complain about you, to make your parents worry about your future."

I felt bad because I wasn't telling Mrs. E. the whole story, so then I told her that for some teachers, like the geography teacher, I don't do the homework.

She didn't seem to care about that. She wanted to talk some more about participation. She asked me, "So when you are not putting your hand up, and you are not giving the answers the teachers are waiting for, what are you actually doing at those times?"

"I am just sitting, doing nothing, maybe listening, maybe not, but I am not disturbing anyone."

"So are you sitting, not disturbing, just being silent?"

She was really getting to me, asking the same thing over and over. This was getting boring.

"Yes, that's what I said, I already told you, that's what I'm doing, just being silent."

And then Mrs. E. said, "Is being silent something you know a lot about?"

Well, that stopped me in my tracks. Because as I have told you, when I was five I didn't speak outside our house; I was silent for more than a year. So silence is something I am expert at, I suppose.

I know I am a quiet person. I don't do small talk, I don't chat. But what about the right to remain silent? How many times do you hear that in police dramas on television? How come criminals have the right to be silent and teenagers don't?

So I said nothing.

One of the things that people don't know about selective mutism is about the fear. I suppose most people know that if you have selective mutism you actually can talk, but you choose to talk only with certain people and in certain places. But what I think most people don't know about us is the fear that makes your heart beat very hard and very fast and everything goes black and you just want to disappear.

It's not only about talking, it is about being looked at, having people listen to you talking and watching you while you talk.

The feeling I used to get, and I can still remember it, when I was expected to speak in front of people who were not my family, or in places where other people might overhear me, was like a big force, a monster, coming down and landing on my neck and grabbing me so I couldn't get away, and squashing my chest down, and I would feel like I couldn't breathe, and I had to close my eyes. I felt as if I could avoid it by not looking at it, and if I didn't look at it, it wouldn't be able to see me either.

My heart used to beat so fast that I thought I would die, because I had heard about heart attacks: my father's father died from a heart attack when I was four, and I thought this feeling was a heart attack and the monster was called the Heart Attacker.

It is really embarrassing to talk about it now, but when I was small, sometimes the Heart Attacker would hide under my bed at night and I was scared to go to the toilet in case he grabbed my feet when I got out of bed.

And that is why I didn't speak at school, because the Heart Attacker would grab hold of me and I couldn't breathe. My parents thought I had asthma but in the end it wasn't asthma or a heart attack, it was selective mutism, but we didn't know it then.

I used to dream that I could fly. I don't mean wishful thinking or daydreaming, I mean real dreams, the dreams you have when you are asleep. I would fly high above all the schools and all the teachers, and people would look up and say, "Look! There goes Amethyst!" And nobody would be able to tell me what to do, nobody could try to make me speak, because I would just fly away.

Selective mutism is a kind of phobia. You can't explain it to someone who doesn't feel it. My dad has no fear of spiders but my grandmother, his own mother, just can't stand them. If she sees one in her flat she actually phones my dad to come over and get rid of it for her. I asked her how it felt to be scared of spiders, and she said, "It's not that I am scared of them, they are just disgusting to me, I can't explain it." And she actually shuddered when she was telling me.

But I could see that her feeling about spiders is not a real phobia, because feeling really disgusted, even shuddering with revulsion, is not the same as the fear people feel if they have a phobia. She doesn't feel terror, and she wouldn't have known what I was talking about if I had told her about the Heart Attacker.

Mrs. E. was still talking about what was going on in school between me and my teachers.

"I wonder," went on Mrs. E., with her pondering expression, hand on her chin, head tilted to the side, "I wonder why it is that after Silence left you alone for so many years, since you were about seven and you stopped coming to speech therapy, it is now trying to make a comeback? What is it that Silence has noticed in your life that makes it think it can come back again?"

I didn't know what to say. This was a new idea for me, to think of silence as a thing, or as a character with a name, not as something that is just – me. And to think of being silent not as something that the Heart Attacker made me do, or (these days) as something I choose to do, my preference, but rather as something that you can give a name to and ask questions about, in the same way that you can name a character in a detective story.

Anyway we had come to the end of the session and I had to leave, and I was glad actually, not because it felt bad talking about this but because it was a whole new idea, and I like to think about my ideas on my own, in my room, and maybe write them down in a Moleskine notebook.

12

The perfection of Moleskine notebooks

School is a problem for me and my real life is totally separate from my school life.

I think I should never have gone to school. I have two reasons for saying this. The first reason is that I was always perfectly happy going around the world with my mother and father and seeing all those places and hearing different languages. I presume that my parents must have decided that when I was five they would have to obey the law and send me to school, because all children from a certain age have to go to school, but in those days I didn't know anything about the law. And the fact is that I learned so much from travelling: so much geography and geology and history, and I got to listen to and sometimes even understand so many languages.

A wonderful thing I learned while on travels with my dad was about archaeology. My dad is sometimes asked to accompany a dig so that they can consult with him about geological issues like different rock and soil types, to help them decide on a date for something they have found, and we often went with my dad to see the dig and to watch them discover new finds. Maybe that is what started me off on my interest in digging and searching and discovering things that have been lost.

These are things that you would probably never learn at school.

The other reason I think school was of no use to me is that everyone says that children have to go to school to learn to read, but I already knew how to read before I started school. I learned to read when we were still travelling with my dad to all those faraway countries and deserts. Every morning, while my dad was at work, my mom and I would find a place to go and sit and have tea or a cold drink and she would read to me and point to each word as she read. I think I must have been about four when she bought me the first of my Moleskine black notebooks and started teaching me the letters and sounds and how they join together to make words.

So I could read even before I started school, and I didn't need to go to school to learn to read. And now, I can find any information I need online and I don't need a teacher to tell me what is already in a text book or what is out there on the Net. I know how to do research; my parents are scientists.

Some children are home-educated, and I wish I could have been one of those children. Now that I have been at school for nine years, I don't actually hate it; I am used to it, but I wouldn't call it fun, and I definitely learn more from travelling with my family than I learn at school.

I haven't told you about my special notebooks. They are not school exercise books, and they are not ordinary notebooks, and nobody at school will ever know about them or see them.

Moleskine notebooks are not made of moles and not made of skin. It is simply a weird name which was given to the books by the manufacturer, who got the idea from a travel writer, Bruce Chatwin. Because my family travel so much, we have lots of books written by people who travel as a job, as a career, and Bruce Chatwin's books are in this collection. I love his book *Songlines* because he describes how he is searching for something that can't really be seen: the historical tracks where aboriginal Australians travelled. The tracks are invisible to strangers, but those people in that culture know where they are and they can see something which the rest of us can't see. They sing the songs in the correct order at the right time and that guides them where to go, where to find water and the important places they need to visit. Their songs are the signs that help them track and find things. And they have been doing this for hundreds of years, so what they see is something from the past which means a lot to them in the present.

When I read Bruce Chatwin's book I thought that what he describes is something like my search for fossils: you know something must be there, and you know more or less where to look, but it is unseen, and if you are not careful, it can be lost forever.

Anyway, in one of his books he describes using a specific kind of notebook on his travels, which he would buy from a shop in France, before the shop closed down and the notebooks were no longer available. He tells the story about searching for this special kind of book, which had been popular in France and which had been used by famous artists, like Picasso and Matisse.

Bruce Chatwin tells how at some stage, someone in France says to him, 'there are no more Moleskine books.' Some people think he just made that name up, and it seems that the present manufacturer of these notebooks had the idea of creating some unusual notebooks and calling them by the name which Chatwin used.

You can buy three notebooks shrink-wrapped into a small parcel. These days you can get the covers in lots of different colours, which I don't like; originally they were available in black, or in un-dyed cardboard, which are lovely if you want to do drawings or doodles on the cover. But I prefer the black ones.

The notebooks have rounded corners and soft cardboard covers. Some of them have an elastic band to hold it closed, and they all have a spine which is sewn, using quite small stitches, and this lets the book lie flat when it is open. And they have a wonderful extra detail: a little expanding pocket inside the back cover where you can keep receipts or tickets or other small paper things you pick up while you are travelling, and that way you can look after the bits and pieces you collect on the way.

So I first saw a Moleskine notebook before I started school, when we were travelling with my dad on his work trips, and my mom bought one when she wanted to teach me to read. I still have those original books of hers, with their letters and beginner reading words in her big neat handwriting. Later, once I knew the letters, she would use the notebooks to write little stories for me, and I would read the stories to my dad in the evening when he had finished his work. My mom is really good at making up stories and I am hoping one day she will find an artist to draw pictures for her stories and she will print them and make them into real books that people can buy and read. But for now, she says, they are her personal family stories and she doesn't want the whole world to read them, just my dad and me and my brother Jasper.

I still use the same kind of notebook for writing at home. You can get different sizes: I buy the ones that are small and can fit in your pocket, so that even if you are travelling you can take your books with you and add your notes whenever you find something important to write down. I have thirty eight of them now, all of them numbered, and each one has a title. I keep them in a chest of drawers in my room and I never leave them lying around; I always put them back in the drawer if I am finished writing. That way I keep them safe and they don't get lost, and nobody gets to see them. Not even my irritating brother Jasper who is always trying to find the combination to the lock I have used, so he can look at my books. Those books have got everything I know written in them.

The titles of the books are the things I am interested in. One is called 'Fossils I have Found' (number 23) and another one, number 31, is 'Hidden in the Landscape.' This Landscape book is for writing down the different signs which archaeologists use to decide where to dig a trench; sometimes it is marks in a field which they see from above, in a plane or helicopter, but sometimes it is a mound in a field which doesn't make sense in the flat land all around it. So the landscape gives you a little hint, and you have to be aware of it and look for the clues; you have to get your eye in, otherwise you would never know to go and look deeper there. This is the kind of detective work archaeologists do. Another notebook is for writing down the titles of all the detective stories I have read.

I also use my notebooks as diaries where I write my new ideas, with the date on which I first thought about that idea. One of the notebooks is for future stuff: specific fossils I still want to find once I become a palaeontologist, or places I want to go to which have special fossil sites, like the West Coast Fossil Park outside Cape Town, in South Africa, or Liaoning in China, which is called the Pompeii of the Mesozoic age, because of the huge number of dinosaur, mammal and plant fossils found buried there in volcanic ash.

I also have a few notebooks, usually the bigger size, where I stick pictures of things I want to look at and to remember. Some of my favourite pictures are of sand dunes in Namibia, because each one is different, and they are always on the move, although not in a time span that you can see in one day or one week; but if you go back to a particular place later it will look different. I also have printouts of things which I have photographed with my USB digital microscope: pictures of granite magnified sixty times, and magnified pictures of sand grains from different places in the world which we have visited.

I only ever use Moleskine notebooks. I never use exercise books with spiral binding, and I don't like stapled books either, because you can never be sure if a page is missing or not and if you pull out a page it is lost forever. When a book is sewn, losing a page is unlikely. At the back of the notebooks, some of the pages have perforated edges, so you can in fact remove a page without damaging the book, and what I like about that is that the counterfoil always stays in the book, like in a cheque book, so you always know if a page has been removed.

I don't like my pages to get lost, because that means something important that I wrote is gone. And I don't like it if someone says, 'Can you just pull out a blank page for me, I need some paper.' My notebooks are not for that.

The books I like cost quite a lot, they are much more expensive than the ordinary exercise books you can buy in any high street shop, but that is what pocket money is for.

13

Granite

This was the third paper I wrote for the English teacher, according to our bargain that she would not expect me to talk in class as long as I could prove to her that I was not just skiving off and being lazy.

Granite

By Amethyst Simons

I have chosen to write about granite because it has become a topic of conversation in our house lately. We have been renovating the kitchen and my parents were trying to choose a material to use for the countertop.

Because my father is a geologist, it is not surprising that they chose stone, and their final choice was granite.

They spent hours choosing the granite, and my dad even took time off work to go with my mom to advise because of his knowledge of geology. They went to several companies before deciding, with my father analysing the colour and the composition and the markings. I think they must have driven the salespeople mad, but eventually they made a choice.

The word 'granite' is derived from Latin, from the word 'granum' which means grain, like a grain of corn.

So the word describes the appearance of the stone: bumpy and grainy. But our piece of granite, our countertop, is polished and is as smooth as a mirror. I do have a piece of granite I picked up on a beach in Cape Town, which is bumpy and rough and grainy, and you can easily see, even without a microscope, the different crystals in it.

Granite is rock made up of different minerals, with at least 20% quartz and up to 65% alkali feldspar. It is formed under special conditions of heat and pressure which are intense enough to melt rock into magma, and this kind of rock is called 'igneous.' These conditions of heat and pressure are found deep underground, and are caused by different events: the plates of the earth colliding, or one plate being pulled underneath another, or the pressure and heat in 'hotspots' such as volcanoes. It is because of this intense heat and pressure, and the combination of the specific minerals, that granite is so strong and so long-lasting. Most of the crust of continents is made of granite.

Granite is known for its strength and hardness, and this has led to the word 'granite' being used in an idiomatic way, to indicate strength of character, or hard-heartedness. Perhaps even hard-headedness.

Sometimes I think that I am a bit like granite. Hard-headed. Or at least that is what is sometimes said about me. I know when I am told this that it is not meant as a compliment, but I haven't yet decided whether I am pleased about being compared to granite, or not.

Because granite is so strong and so hard, it is sometimes used as blocks and as flooring tiles in public buildings. There is a city in Scotland, the city of Aberdeen, where nearly all the main public buildings are made of granite.

Granite is also used for tombstones, monuments and memorials because it is so long-lasting. I like to think of memorials being made to last, because I think it is important that the names of people who are now dead are never forgotten. You can't remember someone if you don't know their name, and engraving a name on a granite memorial is one way to help people remember them. Names are important.

The particular granite my mom and dad chose for our kitchen has big chunks of blue feldspar crystals, which reflect the light where the stone has been polished. It is called Blue Pearl granite, because of the blue feldspar, but the background is almost black. My mother says she chose it because it is beautiful but also because of its strength.

When I asked my father for the scientific name of this particular granite he told me it is actually not a granite but a syenite, and this means that it is almost the same as granite but only has small amounts of quartz in it. The fact that they chose syenite for the kitchen is important because it is an example of how a detective may find a kind of clue when he is searching to link up facts which don't seem to go together. I will tell you in a little while why syenite is, for me, a clue.

My favourite piece of granite is Cleopatra's Needle, which is strangely named, because it is obviously not a needle, and it also had nothing to do with Cleopatra. It is an obelisk: a huge vertical column of rock, twenty one meters high, engraved with hieroglyphics. It now stands in London on the bank of the river Thames, close to Embankment Tube station.

An obelisk is a tall, four-sided column, narrowing as it gets higher, and forming a pyramid shape at the top.

Because I like words and I think names are important, I will tell you what this kind of monument was called by the Ancient Egyptians who created it: 'tekhenu.' The Ancient Greeks called them 'obeliskos' and our English word is derived from Greek.

I said previously that it was relevant that my parents chose syenite for their kitchen countertop, and now I will tell you why I think that it is a kind of clue, if you are the kind of person who likes tracking and searching for information. Cleopatra's Needle is actually not made of granite but of syenite. Most people wouldn't know or care about this; to them granite is granite if it looks like granite. Most information you read about Cleopatra's Needle says it is made of granite, and I thought so too, until I did some more research. But words are important, and being accurate is important, if you are a scientist.

In Egypt today, near Aswan, you can still see an unfinished obelisk at the syenite quarry. This obelisk was apparently abandoned when a crack appeared in its surface, and it was never completed. It is still lying there, horizontal, connected to the surrounding rock. We went there on one of our desert trips with my dad, a few years ago.

The origin of the word syenite is the ancient name for Aswan, the city in Egypt where the quarries are to be found. Aswan used to be called Swennet in ancient Egyptian and Syene in ancient Greek. That may be a completely irrelevant and boring fact for most people, but for me it is the kind of coincidence that leads me to new discoveries. I am like a detective: no information is too irrelevant, and chance discoveries can lead to you finding the answer to a problem. The fact that our *countertop, which was so carefully chosen, and the obelisk at Embankment, which is my favourite piece of large rock, are both made of the same stone, is an important coincidence. Maybe all it shows is how a child's personality and tastes can be influenced by their parents, even if they are not aware of it. Or maybe it is telling me that there is something important about that syenite obelisk in the quarry – perhaps there is a message there that I need to be able to find the meaning of.*

Maybe there is no such thing as a chance coincidence.

Cleopatra's Needle was carved in Egypt around 1500 BC but at some stage it fell over, with the hieroglyphic writing face down, into the dry desert sand. It was a kind of burial which preserved it, and protected the hieroglyphs from being worn away. It is in a way similar to how fossils are preserved in sandstone, or how human bodies can be preserved in peat, like the 2000-year-old 'Lindow Man' who was found preserved in a peat bog in Northwest England. Even though fossils and Lindow Man are preserved by completely different kinds of processes.

This obelisk was presented to Britain in 1819 by the ruler of Egypt, but for some reason it was only brought to the UK in 1878.

So the hieroglyphs were protected by the desert sand and climate until the obelisk came to England. Things have not been so good for it since then, because on this piece of rock you can see that even though granite is a very hard material, suitable for monuments and memorials, which need to last, it can be damaged and worn away. This is called weathering. The minerals react to acids in polluted rain, and both granite and syenite will eventually erode.

I think it is very sad that the hieroglyphs engraved on this stone lasted for thousands of years while being preserved in the dry unpolluted sand of the Egyptian desert, but in less than two hundred years the British pollution and acid rain have been eroding the engraving. Maybe a change of place is not a good thing; perhaps things should stay where they originally were and not be damaged by moving them around the world.

There is something else which I love about Cleopatra's Needle, and that is the number of stories it can tell us. Some of the stories are ancient, and some are more recent.

There is the story of the rock itself, as ancient as the earth: the story about how it was formed, and about its qualities and how it lasts, or how it weathers.

Then there is a second story, which is about the people in Egypt who created this obelisk, who cut the stone and shaped it, and who engraved it over three thousand years ago. This story is told by the hieroglyphic writing: it tells us about the people who lived there at that time, what they thought and believed.

Then there is the more recent story, a third story, about how this obelisk was finally brought to London, because it took years of argument about how to transport it and who would pay for it. And when it was finally being brought here, the ship was damaged in a storm and several of the crew were drowned. There is a brass plaque at the base of the pedestal which tells that story and commemorates those sailors.

So the stone, which was originally created as a tribute to two Pharaohs, so that they would be remembered, became a triple memorial: to the age of the stone, to the stone masons who carved it, and to the sailors who brought it here.

Perhaps you should count the tribute to the two Pharaohs as a story too, so that makes four.

But there is more to it; there is another story. The fifth story is this:

When the obelisk was put up in London, in 1878, a time capsule was hidden in the pedestal. It contains a very strange collection of things: some photographs of people, including a portrait of Queen Victoria, some cigars, some toys, some bibles, a map of London, a railway timetable, as well as a written version of the story of the complicated and disastrous transport of the monument from Egypt to England.

So that makes Cleopatra's Needle a quintuple memorial.

I wonder who it was who chose which objects to bury in the time capsule. Whoever it was must have thought that these represent everything you need to know about what people were thinking and doing in 1878. Just as the hieroglyphs help us know what people were thinking around 1500 B.C.

And I wonder if, in maybe a thousand years' time, some archaeologist will come and dig it up and try to make sense of the objects, because by then the hieroglyphs will have eroded completely, and people will have to judge what this memorial was for by the strange collection of objects buried underneath it. Whoever digs it up would be someone like me, a person who likes to find buried treasure and to learn about the past from what can be found.

This is how memory works. Memory is usually thought of as something we carry in our minds. But

*things can carry a memory too; they can tell a story long
after the people involved are dead.*

Mrs. E. asked me to bring her a copy of a paper I was
writing for the English teacher, so that we could talk
about whether I wanted her to help me with written
work or whether we should work on something else.
She asked me what I thought, but I didn't actually know
what to suggest, because it wasn't my idea to come and
see her and I really didn't feel like talking any more about
my problems, my Attitude, my sullen face or anything
else that everyone was bugging me about.

So I gave her my paper on granite, and I played
Codewords on my phone while she read it.

"Hmm," she said. "Granite. This is very new to me,
I didn't know anything about granite. Is geology
something you know quite a lot about?"

Well, surely she knew that my dad is a geologist.

"Does Jasper know as much about it as you do?"

"No, he is interested in his own things, his computer
and maths and magician's tricks."

"So you have a special interest in this subject.
I suppose not many students of your age know this much
about rocks?"

I thought, you could say that again. But I didn't
say it.

She went on. "You wrote about how strong granite
is, and that is why your mother chose it for her countertop, and that is why it is used for memorials. And you
also said – now where is it? Oh, here it is: '*Sometimes
I think that I am a bit like granite. Hard-headed.*' Now,

I am curious... could there possibly be other ways to use the word 'granite' to describe people?"

I didn't know what she meant.

"I mean about its being hard as well as strong. Are all strong things also hard things? Is there a difference between hard and strong?"

I thought about that and said yes, but she wanted an example. So I said, "Like a person being able to lift weights, he is strong, but he may also be kind, or friendly, so he is not a hard person."

Then Mrs. E. said, "You say here in your paper that some people call you hard-headed. But I wonder if maybe the other quality of granite, its strength, might describe you too?"

I said nothing, just looked at her. What was she getting at?

"Do you think you are strong? Can you think of something you do that shows how strong you are?"

"Well, I am not giving in to the geography teacher, I am not going to do homework for him, I don't care what punishment the school gives me. I am strong that way," I said.

I know I have told you that Mrs. E. is not like other teachers, and in fact she isn't really a teacher at all, she is a speech therapist and a coach and a counsellor. And she just didn't seem to care if I did homework or not, and she didn't try to persuade me to do geography homework; in fact she seemed to be encouraging me not to do it, because she said, "Yes, I can see that you are strong in that way, a person does need to be quite strong to resist the demands of teachers and their punishments. Any other examples of being strong?"

I thought and thought. I know it was physical strength and fitness that got me to finish the cross-country run ahead of some of the boys in my class, but I didn't think Mrs. E. was talking about physical strength now.

I remembered how I stood up for Jasper once, a few years ago, when some boys in the playground were bullying him. Mrs. E. made me explain exactly what happened: who was there, how it felt, and how I got the boys to leave Jasper alone, not just on that day but for weeks and months afterwards.

"Hmm," she said, chin on hand, "so your strength helps you do some things. What does that say about what is important to you, about what your strength helped you to do? What was it you were doing for Jasper?"

"I was protecting him."

"So maybe this is what is going on at school. It seems that protecting is something you are rather good at, something that is really important for you to do. So I am wondering, what other things do you protect?"

I thought about my fossils, my Moleskine books of ideas, my dictionary. What did that have to do with all the fuss the teachers were making, what did that have to do with anything? Anyway I like to keep my school problems separate from everything else in my life.

I kind of saw, somewhere far away, that she was trying to show me something, but I couldn't see what it was. I couldn't get my eye in yet.

14

Looking and losing

There is something you need to do if you are searching for a thing which is not immediately visible. I call it 'getting your eye in' and what I mean by that is a specific state of mind; it is not just something you do with your eyes.

Once you get your mind into a 'search state', your eyes start to work in a new way, and they see things you couldn't see before; they see patterns and regularities and sometimes, suddenly, something new.

Since I was really young, I have been trained by my parents in how to look at details. My dad was always teaching me about the rocks and their layers; if you look really carefully you find clues to how old they are and their chemical properties. He showed me how layers of sand get compressed to make sandstone, and how the layers remain visible, and how some rocks turn red because of iron. You look at the layers, their regularity, their thickness, their colour; you keep looking and looking until you can make sense of what happened to those rocks.

Sand needs to be looked at even more carefully. Sand is not the same wherever you go. My dad taught me that if you study sand in detail, microscopically, you can understand how it is that giant dunes can keep their shape without collapsing, even though a handful of sand collapses onto a table and doesn't keep a shape. He showed me the differences between types of sand, and how that affects the way sand moves, and it explains why you find only certain kinds of sand in sandstorms, while other kinds of sand are found in different places on the earth. And he showed me how it is that you can mix two different kinds of sand, and when you pour them out onto a surface, they separate themselves into their different grain sizes. You can try it out: mix some sugar with fine beach sand, shake it up, and then pour it slowly into a pile on a table.

My mom taught me to look carefully too: she was always telling me to look around, when we were travelling, and to notice the different kinds of plants growing in each area, and the different kinds of clouds. When she was at university she studied botany. She would tell me about the people who lived in the country we were visiting, and show me what crops they grew and what they liked to eat, and we would walk in the markets and see what they were selling.

My mom loves to buy pieces of printed fabric and woven cloth from each place we visit, and she has a collection which she uses as tablecloths or curtains or pillowcases or just to look at and touch. She can tell you what kind of weaving it is, and what kind of dye was used to make the colours, and what kind of plant was used to make the threads to weave the material. She would go to the weavers' houses and watch them weave, and look at the warp and weft with a magnifying glass to try to see more clearly, to see the type of thread and which pattern they were using, and she would help me to see how each one was very subtly different from the others, and sometimes you could identify the style of the maker, as individual and unique as a fingerprint.

This was another time when I realized how important names are. Before I knew about warp and weft, I just saw a piece of cloth. After my mom taught me those names, I started to see things I simply hadn't seen before: how the different arrangements of warp and weft can make different patterns, like herringbone or checks. It was the names that helped me to see them. Looking is not just about eyes; it is about naming and then looking again when you know what you are looking for.

At our next session, Mrs. E. went back to my paper on granite. She pointed to the place where I wrote about how I like to find the origin of words and where I explain the origin of the word 'granite.'

"I wonder…" she started off, as usual, with her pondering look.

I already knew I had better sit up and listen because when Mrs. E. does that you know something is about to come at you. Something you never thought about before: a new idea.

"I wonder," she continued, "Could it be that finding the origin of a word is a bit like finding a fossil? Something that was lost, that you manage to retrieve? Or recover?"

I looked hard at her. For a moment I couldn't breathe. Other than that first paper I wrote for the English teacher, I had never talked to anyone about my feelings about finding things that were lost. I had certainly never talked to anyone about my list of '*re*' words. To find out that Mrs. E. knew those things about me was a surprise, because I haven't really met any adults who actually understood that about me. So I told her about my dictionary. I told her I like to know where words come from because the more you know about the word, the more perfectly you can use the word. And I told her the subtitle of my dictionary, which is *The Perfection of Words*. Once you find the right word for a thing, once you have named it, and once you have found out the origin of the word, you know a lot about it, and it is like having a treasure you have found and can keep safe.

She wanted to know more about words, and what you can do with them once you know a lot about their origin and what they mean. She asked me for an example of an interesting discovery about a word, so I used as an example the kind of notebooks she always used when she was making notes during our sessions: 'Foolscap.'

When I first saw the word 'Foolscap' printed on the outside of her notepads, it was a new word for me. I looked it up and found out that it was the name given, a few hundred years ago, to a kind of paper which had a watermark on it, and the picture on the watermark was a cap of a court jester: a fool's cap. So I wrote 'foolscap' in my dictionary because it is a word I like and I told Mrs. E. that that is the kind of interesting discovery you can make when you really look carefully at the origin of a word.

She asked me if I had other strategies like *The Perfection of Words*, so I told her about how I keep my ideas organised. I told her about *The Perfection of Spaces*, which helps me to keep things in the right place, and to know what belongs in which space; how nothing gets mixed up. This is a strategy I use for my fossil collection.

"So I can see that perfection is also something you know quite a lot about," said Mrs. E. "Could you tell me some more about that? I know you have been to so many different countries. I wonder if you might tell me about some of the places you have been to, which are perfect?"

I thought for a while, and I told her about the perfection of the sea and the bougainvillea and the sun on the Greek island.

I also told her about the perfection of an ammonite fossil: its curves, its chambers, and how they are still there, millions of years later.

She asked me to tell her about other perfect things; things that I have found, or seen. I told her about the perfection of the stripes on a zebra, how the black and the white contrast so perfectly, and how each zebra has its own perfect pattern, unique to each animal. I told her about the perfection of the blue feathers of a jay, and the surprise of the black and white stripes on the jay's flight feathers: stripes which are hidden when the wings are folded and which you suddenly see only when the bird flies away. If you are looking carefully.

"I can just picture that," said Mrs. E., "I can see how beautiful these things must be, and how perfect." And she asked me to bring to the next session a few of my most perfect fossils, and also some photos from the island, to show her.

I remembered that when I still had selective mutism, and I was still going to her every week for speech therapy, she once showed me something about perfection. I was about to have my sixth birthday, and she suggested that I sing a song to myself for my birthday.

I thought it was weird, because I wasn't speaking much then, so singing seemed a totally crazy idea, and anyway who would sing a song to themselves on their own birthday? But as usual I remained silent because in those days I was silent most of the time.

Maybe I was waiting for her to explain, or maybe I hoped she would forget about this idea and we could play another game.

She taught me a song called 'Fifteen Animals', and she even had a book to go with it. I loved that book. It is about someone who has lots of pets, fifteen of them in fact, and all the pets in the book, and even the children of those pets, are called Bob.

So even though there are fifteen animals, they are all called Bob.

Mrs. E. said, "This is a perfect song for you, because all the words are the same: 'bob, bob, bob,' you don't have to use lots of words for that song." So she would sing the song, and each time the name 'Bob' came up, she would be silent and I had to do something to fill in the gap. Before I was willing to speak, she suggested that I could just 'bob' my knees and that would stand for the word 'Bob'; later when I started to speak in her sessions, I would say 'Bob' each time she left a pause in a line, and it wasn't too hard because when you only have to say one word, and it is the same word each time, you get used to it and it isn't anything special. So that was when I discovered that a song can be perfect.

By the time I finished speech therapy, about a year later, I could sing the whole song and lots more, and I spoke at school like anyone else. But at the time when she taught it to me, that song was perfect. The right amount of funny, the right amount of talking (very little) and just cute.

Now I think about it, I must have been a funny-looking kid in those days, with funny habits and funny fears, but not funny in a ha-ha way, if you know what I mean.

I have an old photograph, a picture of me in my first year at school. I don't know why I keep it; my mother says she loves it, but I look at it and see a frightened child, hair badly cut, spikes all over the place, and huge staring eyes. I don't remember having that photo taken; it is a school photo, with the name of the school written on the back, so it must have been taken at one of those annual photo sessions they used to have. I have seen that look in the eyes of a tiny wild buck, a *dassie*, caught by a hunter somewhere in Africa and kept in a cage in the market.

So just in case you are thinking that our time together in speech therapy when I was a selective mute was fun and jokes and songs and games, you are wrong. Most of the time it was hard for me. Maybe it was also hard for Mrs. E. too, I don't know, but that was her job and she must have liked it, otherwise she would have gone and done some other job.

"So now I am thinking about things being perfect," said Mrs. E. "What if you see something perfect, maybe a perfect fossil, somewhere in a cliff, high up, and you can't get to it?"

"Then it's lost."

"So a fossil can be lost, and I suppose all those which are still buried in the cliffs and under the earth are still lost, at least until someone finds them."

Then she said, "I am interested in what other kinds of things can be lost. Can the word 'lost' be used to describe something else, something that is not an object? Something that is precious, maybe a time you remember, or a special feeling, that can get lost?"

I thought about those days, years ago, before I turned five, when my mom and dad and I used to travel around the world, and how she used to read to me and take me to markets, and we used to learn about the people who lived in those places and see animals and eat different food, and it was just the three of us, no Jasper to irritate me, and most important, no school to take me away from all the that, to make me do things I didn't want to do. That was a loss, for sure. But I didn't want to tell her about that, it was too private.

So this time it was my turn to say 'Hmmm' because I couldn't think of anything to tell her.

15

The perfection of tea

Mrs. E. went to put the kettle on for tea, and when she came back, you could see that she was thinking. Then she looked at the paper on granite again because she wanted to see what I had written about the desert sand protecting the hieroglyphs.

"Do you know what interests me?" she said. "It is how those three words, 'granite' and 'protect' and 'lost', decided to make an appearance in our session today, together. What is it about those three words that makes them want to be together?"

Well, I was getting used to Mrs. E. talking about words as if they were alive, as if they could think for themselves, and have wishes or make decisions, like a person. She had already done that with Silence, when she asked why I thought Silence had decided to make a comeback since I started the new school.

She drew three circles on a page, and in each one she wrote one of the three words: 'Granite', and 'Protect', and 'Lost', and she drew lines to join them all together, like a triangle.

Then Mrs. E. wanted to know, "Can you think of a time, in class perhaps, or at home, or on holiday, when you used your strength to protect something, to prevent it from getting lost?"

I remembered a discussion in class: they were talking about the rights of children, and the other kids in the class were being silly, about the right to stay up all night, and the right to play computer games as much as they wanted to, and I wanted to tell them about the time when we were in Africa and we saw a child who was a child soldier. He must have been only eight or nine, with a gun, and an army uniform, and I wanted to say what about the right of a child to be a child. But I didn't know how to interrupt and make my voice heard, and the more I thought how terrible and how important this thing was, the worse I felt about saying it.

I should have said it; I should have stood up for my idea in front of everyone in the class, but I didn't; I said nothing.

"And if you had stood up for your idea, if you had made people listen to it, what would have happened to that idea?"

"It would have been protected, it wouldn't have got lost. The only way I could make sure it wasn't lost after what happened was to write it in one of my notebooks at home, the ones where I write my new ideas."

"So," said Mrs. E., "You used your strength to protect Jasper from being bullied, and you used your strength to protect your idea, by writing it down and keeping it safe, even if you weren't, on that occasion, quite strong enough to say it to the class. I am curious: what does that tell you about how you feel about things being lost? If you can save something precious from being lost, what does it mean to you?"

She doesn't give up easily, Mrs. E.

❧

After she talked to me about granite being strong, about the quality of strength in a person, I remembered a day when I found strength. I must have been six and a half. We were on a school trip to the Science Museum. It was a place I had been often; my parents would take me there at least once a month, because they are both scientists.

The best part about this trip was something I had looked at before but had never tried: it was the echo chamber. You put your mouth at the opening of this giant pipe, and I mean giant, you could drive a bicycle down it, and you shout, and your voice comes back to you as an echo.

I stood aside for quite a long time, watching all the other kids, who had no Heart Attacker and who could just talk whenever, shouting and calling into the tube and hearing their echo.

My teacher was encouraging me to have a turn, and I wanted to, I desperately wanted to, but I also didn't want to. It was just impossible, to make a loud noise, in front of everyone, in that big place, and even worse to have to hear my own voice coming back to me – to be scared twice!

So for a while I stood around, and listened to the others, and then I crept closer and closer to the tube, but I didn't dare ask anyone to move aside. I didn't want to take a space in the queue and have to make the big decision and actually have to do something; not with everyone watching and expecting me to do it.

I remember thinking then of Winnie the Pooh. I was reading the Pooh books at the time because my teacher, when I was still in Year Two, gave them to me to read. In fact I still love them, because I think each character in those books is a metaphor for feelings I often have, and for all I know lots of people have those feelings but I wouldn't know because I don't talk to anyone about my feelings – about being nervous and pretending not to, like Rabbit, or about being greedy for delicious sweet things like Pooh, or just feeling silly and bouncy like Tigger.

Anyway, when Pooh is confused or worried or scared he makes up little hums which he hums to himself to express how he is feeling, and sometimes it makes him feel better. Perhaps my teacher chose that book for me deliberately, to give me a little hint that you don't have to go from quiet to loud in one leap; you can use quiet little hums as an in-between step between being silent and talking to other people. Perhaps Mrs. E. had told my teacher about the *Strategy of Small Steps*. So I tried a tiny little hum, with my mouth firmly closed. But it wasn't loud enough to make an echo.

I took a deep breath, and I did a breathing exercise that Mrs. E. had taught me and which we had practiced, and I took another breath and kind of imagined that not only Pooh, but also all the fifteen animals from the birthday song were all sitting next to me, encouraging me to be strong and to use a strong voice. I tried to imagine that they would say it with me so we could be strong together, and then I said "BOB" from the 'Fifteen Animals' song, quite loudly, and it echoed right back at me, and I wished Mrs. E., or at least Winnie the Pooh, had been there to hear it.

But what happened then was amazing, because a few children standing near me liked my word, and they copied me. And then the echo copied them, and they did it again, and I did it again, and then we were all making silly noises and I was copying their noises, and the echo tube was copying us all, and it was so funny.

So I did it. I made a big noise, right there in front of the children in my class and my teachers and in front of all those people who I had never met who were visiting the museum too, and in front of the echo machine which sent my loud voice right back to me.

That was more than a little step for me; it was a really giant step, and by the end of that school year I was talking in class quite a bit, and I was singing along in assembly, and I joined the afternoon science club and there were five other children there, and I could talk to them while we did science.

I think Mrs. E. must be addicted to tea, because we never got through a session without her saying, "I think it is time for tea."

Actually it is something I like, because it reminds me of when my dad sometimes has meetings in our home with his team. They are all sharing what they know; there isn't any one person being the boss. They talk when they want to and they can be silent if they need to think, and if they have nothing to say they say nothing. And they always have something to drink; my father makes them tea or coffee or a cold drink, and I think that is a clever thing to do because it makes people feel they are relaxing in the space together, and they don't have to worry about being 'team players'; they are just all there, working.

I learned a lot about tea from Mrs. E. She is very particular about what kind of tea she drinks. It has to be

Orange Pekoe, with the leaves of a particular size, not too small; tea bags are her pet hate. Although you can now buy teabags which contain whole leaves in them, Mrs. E. is yet to be convinced. She told me she had visited tea plantations and saw that the tea in tea bags was not good quality tea. She always uses the same teapot which has a special cover to put over it to keep the tea warm, and we have to wait the correct amount of time for the tea to draw, even if we are in a hurry or really dying for the tea.

We drink it without milk; that way you get the real taste of the tea. I will never understand how people can bear to ruin their tea by adding milk.

So one day, while Mrs. E. was getting the tea, I was just looking around at the pictures on her wall and I saw something new. It was a framed certificate. At the top it said, in beautiful Italic script,

Guardian of the Memory

I wanted to see what it said below, but the writing was quite small, so I stood up to read it. I didn't think Mrs. E. would mind if I read it, because it was in a public place on her wall. What the certificate said, in smaller letters, was this:

This is to certify that

B. Edelstein of London, United Kingdom

has been registered as the Guardian of the Memory of

Ignace Edelstein

a victim of the Holocaust.

That is when I read his name for the first time.

I thought it must be someone in her family, because of the surname. Mrs. E. came in with the tea, and she saw me reading it. I didn't want to ask, because suddenly I thought maybe it was private after all, but she had seen me reading it, and while we had our tea she told me about him.

He wasn't someone in her family at all, or at least she didn't think so. His was a name she found when she went onto the website of Yad Vashem, the Holocaust memorial organisation. She had read that you could be allocated the name of a person who was killed in the Holocaust, and you would be the guardian of that person's memory. You would be someone who remembered that person, who honoured his memory, because perhaps there were no family or friends to remember him.

I liked the idea that even though Mrs. E. hadn't known this person, and this person was from another country and not even part of her family, he could still be remembered by someone.

On this website, the Yad Vashem website, they have a long list of names you can choose from; in fact it is about six million names, because six million Jews were killed in the Holocaust. So how do you choose one name from so many? Mrs. E. told me she didn't actually choose the name, it came up at random when she went onto the website and asked for a name she could commemorate.

At first she thought that this particular name, the same as her surname, had popped up precisely because it was the same as hers, but when she asked some friends to try the website, they got all kinds of different names. So it must have been a chance coincidence.

Maybe there is no such thing as chance coincidence.

Anyway, she told me that she was quite touched to have been offered this person, with the same surname as her own, and who knows, it could have been someone in her distant family.

And even if it wasn't someone from her family, she explained to me, and it was really unlikely that there could be someone in her family that she hadn't known about, he was a person with whom she suddenly felt a connection, because there was his name, the same as her own.

I think that finding someone with the same name as your own is maybe like seeing someone who is wearing the same T-shirt as you, or who is reading the same book as you on the bus. You feel a kind of connection.

16

Gemstones

I looked up the surname, Edelstein, in the online word translator. The word felt in some strange way familiar, and not just because of Mrs. E.

And of course, it was familiar, because when I looked up the meaning of the two German words, 'edel' and 'stein', guess what they mean?

Literally, beautiful stone. Gemstone.

Like ruby. Or diamond. Or Amethyst.

I was surprised that this had never occurred to me before. Even though I had by now known Mrs. E. for many years, and even though I love to find the origin of words, I had never thought about what her name might mean.

We were all, all three of us, named after precious stones and minerals.

And that meant that there was a connection between us, between me and Mrs. E. and Ignace Edelstein, and maybe for that reason we could all be in some way guardians of each other, and we had a responsibility to each other.

I thought about what Mrs. E.'s responsibility to me might be. That was easy. Mrs. E.'s responsibility was to be my speech therapist. When I was five, she was the person who helped me get rid of the Heart Attacker, and she was the guardian of my silence and my speaking. And now that I am thirteen, she is the guardian of my classroom participation and of my learning how not to infuriate my teachers. Maybe to get them to stop irritating me too.

I remember that when I was still a selective mute, after a few months of going to speech therapy with Mrs. E., we started playing games where I had to say a few more words. I guess by then Mrs. E. must have felt that I would agree to play games where I would be talking to her just a little. And it did feel okay to me; maybe it's just that I was used to her by then, and also I knew she wouldn't make me do anything I didn't want to. She always warned me before any new game; if it was a game that included talking, she would say something like, let's see how the game goes, and if you don't like it we can choose something else.

I actually liked some of those word games, even though I did have to talk, because as I already told you, I do like words, and even when I wasn't talking at school I still knew how to read and spell lots of words and had started writing my own dictionary.

Mrs. E. and I used to play a memory game with pairs of identical multicoloured pictures. You have to place them upside down on the table, all mixed up, and then turning over two at a time you try to find two identical pictures; if they don't match, you put them back, upside down, and the next person has a turn. The talking part involved saying the name of the picture you had turned over. We had a similar game at home, with much more boring pictures, and Jasper used to win this game every time. I could see he had a strategy but he refused to tell me what it was. So at that stage I still couldn't find a way to remember the exact position of the pictures that we had seen and replaced. Then one night, before I went to sleep, when I was re-arranging my fossils in their compartments, I had an idea: to organise the pictures like the little tool boxes, in lines, so each picture would be in its own position in the line; you could remember the place and that would help you remember the picture.

I didn't know how to tell Mrs. E. about my idea. I didn't know the words to use and I didn't want to say so many words to her, but I wanted her to know my new strategy. So at the next speech therapy session I tried to tell her about my strategy, but I felt myself starting to breathe too fast and it felt bad, like the Heart Attacker was squashing my chest.

So what I did was, I put my hand up, like a stop sign, so she would know that I wanted to stop playing and needed a break. And she said, "Oh, I understand, you want to stop playing", but I shook my head 'no' because I didn't want to stop playing and I didn't want her to go and make tea. I wanted to tell her my idea but I couldn't get my mouth to open and I couldn't find the right words. So I started to silently arrange the pictures in rows and columns.

Now I know that the words I needed were 'rows and columns' or even the word 'grid', but then, I was only five, and it was easy to show her but not easy to tell her.

Mrs. E. waited, saying nothing.

This is what I mean about her being my guardian. She always knew when she should stop speaking. Some adults used to think that if I didn't speak, they should speak more and more until I joined in. But the very opposite would happen: the more they talked the more I wanted to get away from them.

Anyway she sat silently while I arranged all the pictures in rows and columns, and then I showed her, by picking one up and putting it back carefully in exactly the same position, how having a special place for each card could help us remember where it was.

I knew she was impressed because she had a huge smile on her face, a real smile, with the skin on the side of her eyes all crinkly. And she said the words that showed me that she understood; she gave me the words I was looking for but which I didn't know. She said, "Oh, I see, it helps us to find the pictures if they are organised in rows and columns! You have made a grid."

And I was so pleased that she understood, and that she thought it was a good idea, that I also spoke then, and I said, "It is like a tool box. Each toy in a special place. Each picture in a special place."

And I told her that my dad kept his stone collections in the same kind of toolbox.

I think if not for Mrs. E. and her strategies, I could have been fossilized too, and maybe I would never have spoken to anyone outside the family. When I got a bit older, and I could talk easily in class and to other people and in the shops, I had a secret idea that one day we would meet again, she and I, and I would say a big thank you to her for helping me get rid of the Heart Attacker who had hung around for such a long time and who messed things up for me so many times.

So you can see how she was a good guardian to me, but what could I possibly be the guardian of, for her? How could I be responsible for her?

It took me a few days to come up with this answer, which I haven't told anyone; it is a private thought.

I think that my responsibility to her is to show people that she is the best teacher, so that even though she is semi-retired, and maybe not many people know who she is, one day, when I am much older, if anyone reads my book, they will hear about her and know what kind of person she was.

Then I thought, putting her in my book is not enough, because right now nobody is allowed to read my books. So in that case, I realised that what really counted was what I chose to do next: if I showed some team spirit at school, even occasionally, or at least participated in a few classroom discussions, the word would get around that it was Mrs. E. who had helped me to do this.

It's not that I think she needs my help in making her famous; I think she is quite happy with her life as it is, but it is something I thought I would like to do. I want to make it clear that I don't think team spirit and classroom participation are in any way important, or relevant, in fact I couldn't care less about those things, but if that is what I had to do to be responsible for Mrs. E. then I would try to do it.

And I also thought, maybe there are other children who have selective mutism and who need help to get rid of their phobia. I read a wonderful book by a boy who had had a school phobia, and he wrote about how it felt and how he got over it, and I think that must have been so helpful to other children who had that problem. So maybe this was one time when I would need to write things down in a book which other people could read, because in a funny way maybe those other children needed me as their guardian, nearly as much as I needed Mrs. E.

But then I thought about Ignace Edelstein. Why would Ignace Edelstein need me to be his guardian? He already had a guardian: Mrs. E., and she is a person who takes things seriously, so I knew she would be a good guardian and would remember him. If anyone asked me to recommend a guardian I would choose Mrs. E., because when I was going to her for speech therapy she was one of the people I trusted most in the whole world.

There was one time, I have to be honest, when I thought she let me down. I must have been about six years old, and I was still going to her for speech therapy every week. It was always in her house. But one day my mother told me Mrs. E. would be coming to school that day, to my class, to see me in class and to visit my teacher.

I didn't like that idea one bit. Mrs. E. was Mrs. E., my speech therapist, not a teacher. She had her office in her own house, she had toys I liked and we had a kind of unspoken agreement that she wouldn't try to make me speak, and when I was with her I never felt that kind of panic, the fear that I felt at school whenever I was expected to talk.

I liked the idea of keeping Mrs. E. quite separate from school, just the way things are kept separate in their compartments in tool boxes and fossil collections. The perfection of places is important to me.

But nobody really asks children for their opinions about things, and even if they did they wouldn't take a five-year-old child's opinions into account, and maybe that's a good thing. So a few days later she walked into the class during a lesson and I wanted to hide under my desk, but luckily she didn't come over to me or even let the other kids in class notice that she knew me. She just sat quietly in a corner during a lesson and at first the teacher didn't take much notice of her and after a while my heartbeat slowed down to normal and I started breathing again.

But then the teacher had to ruin it; she suddenly said, "Amethyst has got a visitor today! Do you want to introduce this lady to us, Amethyst?"

Everyone turned around to look at me, and this teacher was staring at me with her smile which was lips only, and I panicked, I couldn't breathe, and they had to take me to the school nurse for my inhaler.

A little while ago, when I looked online about how speech therapists work with children with selective mutism, they said that it should be done in the school, not at home or in the speech therapist's office, because it was better that way: you work on the person's fear in the place where that fear lives, not in another, different, safe place, because then there is nothing to work with. But not everyone agrees; there are different methods and different ways to do speech therapy. So maybe she was doing it for a reason, and her visit to my class was not designed to make me lose trust in her, but to take me onto the next step. Though at the time it felt like it was designed to make me fall all the way down the stairs.

17

Learning to breathe

After I saw the certificate in memory of Ignace Edelstein, I couldn't get it out of my mind. For the next few days I kept thinking about what it would mean to be a proper guardian, a responsible guardian. The dictionary said 'responsibility' meant being answerable, being reliable and dependable. I liked the fact that I had found two more 're' words, *responsible* and *reliable*, and I added them to my list even though their meaning was not the same as my original 're' words.

Although maybe they did connect: if you *reclaim* something, *retrieve* it, you are showing yourself to be *responsible* and *reliable*.

But in the case of being responsible for the memory of a person who is dead, I think it is a bit different. Because when you are responsible for a living person, like I am supposed to be when I babysit my brother Jasper even though he is the most irritating person I have ever met, then that person notices what you are doing. But a dead person doesn't know, can't know, what you are doing for him, so you have to make it up, to do the thing that seems responsible in your own eyes, and only you will know about it.

I asked Mrs. E. what she had to do to be the Guardian of the Memory of Ignace, and she said, to light a candle in his memory once a year, on Holocaust Memorial Day.

It didn't seem enough.

⁂

The certificate on Mrs. E.'s wall also gave the date on which Ignace Edelstein was born: It said '*Born Constantinople 16.02.1903.*' And his date of death: '*Died in Auschwitz 14.07.1942.*'

So he was thirty-nine when he died.

I tried to think of anyone I knew who was thirty-nine. My dad is forty-one, so that is nearly the same age. I tried to imagine what it would be like for my dad to die but I couldn't let myself think about that.

Was Ignace a dad? Did he have children who got left behind when he was taken, who grew up without a living dad?

I just couldn't see how Mrs. E. could guard the memory of Ignace Edelstein when nobody knew anything about him.

⁂

I was still going to Mrs. E.'s house once a week, and we would work on different things: sometimes the homework which I was not keen to do, or some research for my English papers.

Then we had a new project. Every Friday, one student in the class would offer to give a talk to the rest of the class on any topic linked to what we were learning at the time. It was voluntary and you will already have guessed that I had never yet volunteered. But now I decided I was going to get the teachers off my back, at least for the rest of the term, by choosing one lesson where I was going to show everyone how I could participate, how I could not only talk in class but actually make a complete speech.

I hadn't felt, for a long, long time, the kind of panic I used to have when I had to speak, but just thinking of having to do this was making me breathe faster and feel a bit panicky. Mrs. E. must have noticed, because she said, "Do you remember the window man?"

I didn't know what she was talking about.

She reminded me that a long time ago, while I was still going to her for speech therapy because I wasn't talking at school, she had invited a man to come and repair her windows because her house was old and the windows didn't fit well and there were draughts in every room.

Then I remembered. I think it was a short time after I started going to her for speech therapy, before I could speak to Mrs. E.

One day, when I was having a nice quiet time at speech therapy, colouring in some little labels I made for the tree house, which would show which dolls lived on which level and which doorbell you had to ring to get a certain doll to come and open the door for you, I heard someone walking in the room above Mrs. E's room.

Before that there had never been anyone around except my mother who would sit with us for a little while at the start of the session and then go and sit in the waiting room and make phone calls to her friends or read or play Patience on her phone.

So when I heard footsteps I thought at first that it was my mother coming back into the room, but I know her footsteps; she always wears the same kind of shoes and they make a very specific sound, and her footsteps are always quick, kind of brisk and snappy, and make a clicking sound on the ground, and she always moves quickly. And this was not her. It was someone bigger, heavier, with big shoes that didn't click. Someone who moved slowly and who was coming down the stairs.

I froze.

I looked at Mrs. E. and she didn't seem to have noticed anything.

It's not that I was scared of people, I don't want you to think that. I wasn't scared he was a robber or anything. I just didn't want him to look at me or talk to me. Mrs. E. carried on pretending she couldn't hear anything so I carried on playing snakes and ladders and not talking. But I couldn't concentrate and I made mistakes counting the numbers on the dice. The footsteps walked past our room; the door was closed so thankfully nobody could walk in and look at me, and the footsteps went towards the back of the house.

Mrs. E. must have seen that I was frozen, because I was being even more still than usual, or maybe she read my mind, so she said, "Don't worry, that is the man fixing my windows. He will be walking around upstairs for a while and sometimes he has to come downstairs to get his tools."

I guess all that may have been one of her strategies too, or at least it became one, because one day she said, "Would you mind if I leave the door of my room open, just in case the repair man needs to call me to check if I am happy with what he has done?"

And that seemed okay. Small steps.

And the next thing she did was to say, "Well, the windows are all fixed now, no more draughts blowing in, do you want to come and help me test them?"

So we took some tissues from the tissue box, and she showed me how to tear them into long strips, and we went upstairs where the man was, and Mrs. E. showed me how to hold a strip next to the closed window, and if it moved or fluttered it meant there was still a draught coming in, but if it stayed absolutely still in our hands it meant the window was properly sealed.

I remember how impressed I was with her strategy of using tissues to check the draughts, and I went around our own house for days after that, checking our windows.

And I wonder today if she had a few strategies going on at the same time; if she had told the window man not to speak to me and not to frighten me, because he just stood aside and said not a word. Mrs. E. and I tried out every single window with our tissue strips, and there were no draughts, and she asked me, right there in front of the window man, if I was sure, and I nodded 'yes' for each window, and then she paid him his money and thanked him and he left.

Of course, even though I don't think that Mrs. E. specially invited the window man to help me get over my phobia, I do know now that she had some careful strategies which she used. I have read about them online, and they are things that speech therapists use to help people like me, with selective mutism. Like getting me to just nod, but still to be seen to answer the question she had asked me, so I was actually communicating in the presence of a new person. Or getting me to walk all around the house, with her and the window man, so that I was taking new steps up the 'staircase of different places', and not just limiting my communication to when I was sitting in her office.

Mrs. E. would say to me, "I know talking is hard for you sometimes. Not at home, but outside your house. But do you know, I know some other children, and talking is sometimes hard for them too."

Well that was interesting for me, not because I used to think 'why me', or anything like that, but because suddenly there was a kind of name for my trouble which was different from Heart Attacker (nobody but me knew about that particular name) but which was a bit easier to think about. Just hearing her say "Talking is hard for you sometimes" made me feel that it wasn't something inside me that was the problem, it was just something that happens to people, and it happened to other people too, not only to me.

Now I realise it was only when she gave my fears a name, when she said "talking is hard" that I started to see that I could think about this thing that was happening to me in a new way. I could look at it carefully, and maybe find a way to get away from the fear, instead of thinking of it as something that was completely out of my control. So I guess being given a name for a problem can make it possible to understand that if something happens to you, you yourself are not the problem; it is the thing that has happened that is the problem.

I started to think that names are important in a whole new way, which I hadn't thought of before.

She also said, "Those other children, they also feel fear when they have to talk. And sometimes the panic makes them feel like they can't breathe, but if they breathe deep and slow, counting to five, and letting the air go out and in slowly, then they may feel better."

And we would do a little bit of practice breathing so I would know how to do it if I needed to. Mrs. E. liked to say, "Be prepared! You may need to use your breathing strategy this week!"

I think it helped to know that I had a strategy to carry around with me, like carrying around an asthma inhaler, just in case.

So now, in High School, while I was preparing to give the Friday talk to the class, she reminded me of the strategy of breathing and we practiced it a few times, just in case I might need it.

18

Strategies of separation

Once I had decided to do the Friday talk to the class, I had to choose in which lesson to do it.

I talked to Mrs. E. about it and we went through the list of every teacher, and every subject, and what was going on in each class. Of course at first I wanted to do it in the English class because my English teacher had no complaints about me and she would have appreciated the effort I put in, knowing how much I hated talking in front of lots of people.

But it seemed like only half a victory, because I was already halfway there with her. I could have just written one of my papers which I was anyway writing for her, and read it to the class; it might be quite easy. But there would be no sense of having changed anything much, and it wouldn't do anything for my reputation as a non-participator.

Mrs. E. agreed that perhaps I wouldn't feel any sense of achievement if I chose the English lesson, it being so easy for me. But it wasn't a sense of achievement I was looking for, because doing this was not a personal goal of mine. It was, I have to be honest, a way to say to them, to the teachers and also to my parents, "Ha! You think I can't do it! You think I can only be sullen, that I have an

Attitude. Well, I will show you that my Attitude is something I can put on, and take off, like a hat, whenever I choose."

So I chose the geography lesson as my test case for participation, because that teacher was the one who hated me. I chose him because I wanted to show him up, but I didn't tell Mrs. E. that.

I wrote the oral presentation at home, and gave it to Mrs. E. to read at our next session. I had written about the Karoo Desert: how it used to be, about three hundred million years ago, not a desert at all, but a huge shallow inland sea with swamps and trees, and how it was now a really wonderful site for fossils of amphibians, many of which are in museums in South Africa. I wrote about the quagga, which was a kind of zebra which lived in the Karoo. The quagga had brown and white stripes, not black and white, and those stripes were only on their necks and heads. They were hunted to extinction in the late 1800's which shows how things can become extinct not just when the environment changes, or when a meteor causes the extinction, but when people hunt things to extinction. I wrote about how the Karoo is actually a semi-desert, not a true desert, and about the best crop being the sheep which can graze on the driest plants. I wrote about the special kind of metal multi-bladed windmills which you see there, which are so typical of the Karoo landscape, and which I think are so beautiful. There is such low rainfall that farmers need to be constantly pumping water out of the ground. I wrote about how the farmers try to start their work before dawn so that by the time it gets really hot, by eleven a.m., they can go indoors and close their shutters and sit in their houses until evening, when it gets a bit cooler.

While Mrs. E. read my speech, I used her computer to look online for some information about Auschwitz, where Ignace Edelstein had died. So when she spoke to me it took me by surprise, because I was so immersed in what I was reading. She said she liked what I had written about the Karoo, and she suggested a few changes in the order of the paragraphs, and asked a few questions about the topic to make sure I hadn't left out anything important.

Then she said, "This is a good paper. Now comes the next task: to decide whether you are going to read it to the class, or whether you want to make a speech, without notes, or with very few notes, like politicians do when they are speaking in parliament."

I wasn't sure how I wanted to do it, so we looked on YouTube, and we watched some parliamentary debates which are broadcast on TV, and we looked at some TED talks online, where you can watch and listen to famous scientists talking about their work.

I decided that reading the speech would be dead boring. It would be no different from just handing out a typed sheet to everyone in the class and telling them to read it. What I wanted to do was to talk without notes, like a politician, like one of those scientists on TED; to have a point of view and to be convincing, so my class (and that teacher!) would sit up and listen.

It took a long time before I was ready to do it, because I didn't know the techniques. We worked on my posture: we looked at the speakers on YouTube who looked powerful, and who looked lively and interesting, and Mrs. E. showed me how they used their posture to show confidence, and also how they used movement as a strategy: walking towards the audience sometimes, and then stepping back. And how they used hand gestures, to look convincing and get people looking as well as listening.

We worked on where I should look while I talked, because it is not just about the talking but about the looking as well. That was a difficult one for me. I still hated having people stare at me, though I knew how to use staring as one of my rudeness strategies. But the kind of eye contact she wanted me to use in my speech was moving my gaze from one listener to the next, very, very slowly, not making any fast movements with my eyes which, she said, can make a person look nervous and unsure of himself.

I never knew there could be so many strategies for giving a speech.

We practiced different levels of loudness, because she wanted to be sure that I would speak loudly enough for the kids at the back of the class to hear me, but not so loud that it sounded stupid. I felt really stupid, talking loudly when it was just the two of us in a room, but she got me to go into the next room, her waiting room, and give the speech from there, and when she couldn't hear me she called from her room to tell me.

Of course being Mrs. E. she didn't do it in the way any normal adult would; she didn't say 'I can't hear you', and she didn't say 'talk louder'; she just sang the 'Fifteen

Animals' song, and the minute my voice was louder than hers she fell silent and listened to me, and when I was talking too quietly she started to sing again. It was totally weird, in fact I would have been embarrassed for her if anyone had heard her doing this, and suddenly I felt in some way protective towards her. But her strategy worked, and I got used to projecting my voice.

So that is how I learned the techniques of public speaking: loudness, posture, pacing and pausing, making eye contact with the audience, the whole thing. Don't think it was quick and easy; it took four weeks, and four sessions with Mrs. E., but I did it.

On the day of the speech it was like a successful stage performance: I did it, and it went well. The geography teacher was pleased and even smiled at me. But the next day my life had not changed; everything was the same, school was boring, I hated P.E. and I spent my time planning my next English paper and my next birthday trip.

After that presentation, Mrs. E. wanted to know how things were going in class, now that I had managed to give a talk to the whole class and had done it well and confidently. Maybe she expected my life would have changed and I would have been transformed into a person who talked all day and spent her life texting and doing P.E. with a bunch of other girls.

"It's the same, nothing new. I am still not participating, if that's what you are asking."

To be fair, to give her her due, she told me she didn't want me to think that she was suggesting I should participate; she was just curious to know if I might consider ever doing it, and what I imagined it might feel like for me, if I ever did it.

I told her that if I spoke in class I was not going to just say what everyone was saying, or what the teacher wanted to hear. I refuse to do that, it is too boring. If I did speak, I would have to give my own opinions, and those are sometimes different from what other people think, and then I would have to explain why I think that, and sometimes I can't put it into words the way I can think it in my head, and then they don't get it and I have to explain again, in different words, and by then nobody is listening. And anyway the teachers have to get through their lesson and there is no time for discussions like that, for people to go into detail about their ideas so that other people can understand and consider what they have heard.

"It sounds to me like you have done it once or twice and it felt very uncomfortable? And maybe people were not listening, and the teacher was moving on so he could finish the lesson in time; am I right? Did it happen a few times?"

Well, that Mrs. E., she reads minds, as I may have mentioned once or twice already.

So yes, it did happen a few times and I had already decided I was never going to go through that again, and if Mrs. E. even tried to persuade me to give it another try I was going to walk out of her room right then and never come back. A prepared oral speech is one thing; talking every day, joining in all the time, just casually without preparation, is another.

⁓

I think keeping things separate is important. I don't mix up the topics in my notebooks, and I don't keep my archaeology finds with my fossils. In palaeontology you have to know how to carefully separate the fossil from its bedrock, so that you can see it more clearly. And I suppose I choose to keep myself separate from the kids in the class, and even if I didn't, they would make sure I am separate from them because I am the weirdest kid in the class.

Thinking about things being separate or together made me remember an activity I used to do with Mrs. E. in speech therapy, when I was just starting to be able to speak to her, all those years ago.

She could see that I was more comfortable if she didn't sit quite so close to me and if she didn't look too directly at me. So she used to sit at the side of the table where we were playing, not directly opposite me, and she was careful to look at the toys and not at me. But one day she took out two puppets and a toy table and chairs, and put the puppets around the table, just the way she and I were sitting. She acted out this scene: the puppets were talking to each other, and slowly one puppet moved closer to the other, until they were face to face. Then the other puppet said, "That's a bit too close!" so the first puppet moved a little further away. Mrs. E. explained to me that I could use these puppets whenever I wanted to, and if she was sitting too close, I could move the puppets apart and she would know she must move, but if I felt okay with it, I could leave them there, or even put the puppets a little closer.

Now I know that what she was doing with that particular strategy of hers was letting me be in control of the amount of separation I needed from her, to slowly learn to feel more comfortable being near her and even talking while she was near.

She had another strategy which had something to do with separation. As I have told you, one of the two 'staircase' strategies was to help me get my voice out of Mrs. E.'s room into the outside world, because it is all very well to be able to speak in speech therapy, during the session, but the real aim was to help me speak in other places, at school and at the shops and in the park.

The game was really simple: I had to choose four toys and put them on the table, and then Mrs. E. would go out of the room and I had to say the name of one toy, loudly enough for her to hear me while she wasn't in the room. Then she would come in and pick up the toy whose name she had heard me say.

It seems like a silly game, and it sounds easy, but it wasn't, because of my fear of talking aloud, and of having anyone outside my own house or, now, outside her room, hearing me speak. So she would ask me to practice saying the words quietly, to myself, while I was alone in her room, and then, when I was ready, I had to say it loudly. And once I could do that, she would move further and further away from the speech therapy room and I had to be even louder. It meant I had to be braver, and louder, the further she moved away, otherwise she wouldn't have known which toys I had named.

Now I am thirteen, I sometimes think about that time, and I suppose if I had to name that strategy, I would call it the *Strategy of Separation*. It helped me to move from saying one quiet word, to saying whole sentences, in a loud voice, with Mrs. E. outside the room. So I was speaking while she was in a separate space. And it helped me separate myself from fear: the fear of people hearing me talk.

19

Ways of remembering

Mrs. E. was still harping on the same theme, over and over. She wanted to know if I could remember any other times in the past when I *did* speak up, when I didn't let Silence stop me from speaking, and if I could remember a time, in the past, when people listened to me. Could I remember a time, any time, not just at school, but anywhere, when I spoke in public, when I did manage to tell someone my idea? She kept on saying to me that she wasn't trying to get me to do anything different in class; she was just interested to know if I had, in the past, ever done it, if I could remember one time when I didn't give up and kept on trying to get people to understand, and in the end they listened.

I told her that maybe I had done it a few times in my previous school, but since moving to the new school I definitely didn't get anyone to listen to my ideas, and I didn't even try. But when she asked me to remember an example from my previous school, I couldn't remember anything specific.

She kept on asking me. Maybe last year, when you were twelve? Maybe when you were eleven? Maybe when you were on one of the birthday trips overseas?

Maybe when you were on one of your summer holidays in Greece, on the island?

I must have been about eight, and Jasper was four, or even less, because I am four and a half years older than he is. We were on the island and we had gone swimming. And suddenly my mother looked around and couldn't see Jasper. Everyone panicked, because he hadn't yet learned to swim properly, and they were all running around looking for him. In those days, I had finished my speech therapy and I wasn't totally silent in public places but I still didn't like drawing attention to myself. But I knew where he was and I was trying to tell people and they weren't listening, just panicking and running around calling Jasper. So I took a deep breath and I shouted, really loudly:

"STOP RUNNING AROUND! I KNOW WHERE HE IS, HE IS SAFE!!"

Everyone stopped in their tracks and turned around to see where this big voice was coming from and they couldn't believe it was from Amethyst who usually said very little, and if she did speak it was usually in a quiet voice.

But I knew that Jasper's favourite place on the beach was near the ticket seller's station, at the entrance to the beach, because even at age four he was interested in numbers, and the tickets had numbers on them, each number printed twice. The seller would tear off one side of the ticket and give it to the visitor to the beach, and he would throw the stubs in a box, and he always let Jasper play with them on condition he didn't lose them. And sure enough there was Jasper, looking at the numbers on the tickets and trying to get the ticket seller to tell him what the numbers were in English and in Greek.

"So what was it that you managed to do to help Jasper, that time when your parents were panicking and nobody knew what to do?"

"I had to really shout at all those adults, and I had to make them listen to me because I knew where he was, and they weren't listening; they thought they knew what to do but they didn't. I first said it in a quiet voice but they weren't listening, they were too busy running and panicking, so then I had to shout."

"And when the people didn't want to listen to you, when they thought you were too young to be sensible and they shouldn't bother with what you were saying, but you kept on at them, you made them listen, what was it that you were doing for Jasper?"

I had to think for quite a long time to find the right way to explain it to her. The only word I could think of was protecting. But it wasn't protecting Jasper, because I knew he was safe. I was protecting the adults, my parents, who were completely hysterical.

"Well," said Mrs. E., "I think when you needed to protect your mother and father, and maybe Jasper too, you used a loud voice, and at that moment Silence knew it must take a back seat, because for sure you weren't silent when you were telling those adults to listen to you!"

I looked at her.

"I wonder," Mrs. E. went on, "I wonder if protecting things, protecting ideas and the people in your family, this idea of guarding and protecting and being responsible for ideas and people, is very important to you? Is this something that someone who knows you very well, perhaps your grandmother, might say is a good way to describe you?"

And that was when I understood what I needed to do for Ignace, to be the guardian of his memory. I had to protect him.

Obviously, I am not stupid; Ignace was dead, he had been murdered, and even if I had been there at the time and knew him when he was alive I wouldn't have been able to protect him from being murdered. Nobody could.

But I could protect him now: I could protect his story, and keep his story alive, and in that way I could be the guardian of his memory. And this time, Silence would not be the way to keep things safe or perfect; this time, like that time when my parents thought Jasper was lost, Silence would have to take a back seat, to bow out, to leave the stage, to move off, to go off to some desert and hang around there until it was needed again.

I have already told you that I like to search for lost things, for things that haven't been seen for a very long time, perhaps never seen by any living person. If Ignace died in 1942, there was probably nobody left living on this earth who had ever met him; and if he had no children, or if all of his family were also killed, there would be nobody left on earth who was his family, and nobody to tell his story.

He was as lost as any diamond buried deep underground, or any fossil covered by a cliff. And my way of being responsible for his memory, the way I could help Mrs. E., and perhaps be responsible for her too, would be to try to find him. Not to rescue him, because it was too late, and anyway nobody could have rescued him, but to retrieve what was lost, to recover, to tell his story, and in that way, to protect his memory.

20

Ways of finding

Another English paper. I hesitated before handing this one in, because it seemed so private, so personal, and I didn't know what the English teacher would think of me. But in the end I had to give her something, and I had written nothing else, so I handed it in.

Searching for Ignace Edelstein
By Amethyst Simons

In this paper I am going to talk about what it means to search for something hidden or lost, when you don't really know what it is you are looking for.

Last year, for my mother's birthday trip, we went to Florence and saw some amazing statues by Michelangelo. There are four statues, all in the same museum, and they are called 'Prisoners' or 'Slaves'. They are only partly carved, actually unfinished, so that they seem to be trying to get out of the rock; in a way, they are enslaved in the rock forever. Perhaps Michelangelo didn't have time to finish them; I prefer to think that he was deliberately showing how hard the marble is to carve, and how strong a sculptor has to be to make something emerge from a rock. Or maybe his aim was to show how strong a slave has to be, just to survive.

For me it was very strange to think how the work I sometimes have to do to get a fossil out of its surrounding rock is in a way like what a sculptor does when carving into marble. So I felt a connection between myself and Michelangelo, and when my family had had enough of the museum and wanted to go and eat, I just wanted to stay there and look some more.

In the guidebook, I read something Michelangelo is supposed to have said. It was about finding something hidden inside the stone that he was working on; it was about how the thing or the figure he was looking for was always already there, inside the stone, and all he had to do was to release it so it could be seen. I wrote it down in a notebook which I carry with me on my trips. What he is supposed to have said is this:

"In every block of marble I see a statue as plain as though it stood before me, shaped and perfect in attitude and action. I have only to hew away the rough walls that imprison the lovely apparition to reveal it to other eyes as mine see it."

So for Michelangelo, what he was finding was not ever really lost; he could see it within the stone, and in his mind's eye it was always there, ready and waiting for him to show it.

But I am looking for a person who I can't see; not in my mind's eye and not in a photograph. Ignace Edelstein is someone I have never met, and I don't know if there is anyone of his family who is alive today. I know nothing about him. Not what he did, what he liked or what he was interested in.

All I know is his name, his date of birth and date of death. And I know where he was born and where he was murdered. And my job, my responsibility, is to find him, to reveal him, and to guard his memory.

But I don't know how you can remember someone you never knew, who you can't picture, and who you know nothing about.

You may be wondering: Why would I care who this person was and what happened to him? I am not related to him. He wasn't famous. He is just one name on a very long list; a list of six million other Jewish people who were murdered in the Holocaust. One name out of six million names.

But for no reason that I can yet explain, I am searching for Ignace Edelstein. And even if I can't yet explain the reason why I am looking for him, why I want to hew away at the walls that are surrounding him and preventing the world from seeing him, I know that I want to do this. And to do it, I will need to have a strategy.

The strategy I have chosen is 'The Strategy of Small Steps.' Michelangelo must have used his hammer and chisels carefully, slowly, so as not to make a mistake. I will use my knowledge of tracking and searching carefully and slowly too, one step at a time.

I have come to believe that there is no such thing as a chance coincidence. Successful detectives have to link up all the clues and information they discover, even suggestions and hints, to make inferences and find what they are looking for.

So to me it seems important that what Michelangelo was doing around the year 1520 is not too different from what some quarry workers were doing around 3000 years ago when they started to carve an obelisk at the syenite quarry in Egypt and abandoned it, and not too different from what I am doing in searching for Ignace Edelstein. Neither Michelangelo's statues nor that obelisk were ever completed; they are only partially released from the rock around them. But you can start to see their shape emerging; in the mind's eye both the statues and the obelisk are identifiable objects, that you can see and name and describe.

I spend a lot of time searching for things: fossils, new words, names of birds. So I know something about the strategy of the search. And even if I never find out everything I want to about Ignace Edelstein, even if my work remains incomplete, I will still be like Michelangelo who created four unfinished statues, or the quarry workers who started to carve an obelisk: those people from the past who created some of the most beautiful things I have ever seen.

I will be like Michelangelo and the quarry workers: I will start with a chisel and a hammer and chop my way, a bit at a time, until I can reveal Ignace to the world so that I, and also other people, can see him.

I bought myself a new Moleskine book and I wrote 'Ignace Edelstein' on the cover. On the first page I wrote his name, the two dates, and the two places: where and when he was born and died. Then I stopped because I was stuck. What do I do next? I needed a more precise strategy. Small steps are all very well, but that is a very general idea and I needed to decide exactly where to start, and which steps to take.

I started in the same way that I start searching for fossils, if I am in a new site. You start by thinking: what do you actually know? What is it about this site, this landscape, that you already know?

So I started with the landscape, with geography, because even though I don't do geography homework, I do, as I have told you, know something about geography. I knew from the certificate that Ignace was born in Constantinople, which is now called Istanbul, in Turkey, and I knew he died in Auschwitz, which is in Poland. So I had two place names to start with, and at some time there must have been a journey from one place to the other. So I drew two circles on the page, one for each place, and drew a pencil line joining them.

It seemed strange, because when I looked it up, I found out that the German army in World War Two didn't have Turkey as one of its targets, and so Jews living in Turkey were not sent to Auschwitz. So how and why did Ignace Edelstein get caught by the Nazis if he lived in Turkey?

I went online and typed in a few words for a new search: 'Turkish born', '1942', and 'Edelstein.'

Bingo. It didn't even take a moment to hew away that particular bit of stone and to find what I needed. Up came a list, titled 'Turkish born Sephardim deported from France during World War Two', and there was his name, on a very long list, alphabetically ordered. Next to his name it said 'Convoy number 3'. And the date on which that convoy left for Auschwitz: 22.6.1942.

A new word for me: Convoy.

And now I knew why he was caught by the Nazis: he had been in France, and not in Turkey, during the war.

I searched some more, and found that the convoy had left from a place called Drancy, and travelled to Auschwitz.

I read some more. Drancy, in Paris, was a detention centre where Jews arrested by the French police and later by the Germans were held before being sent by train to Auschwitz. Between 1941 and 1944, Jews were sent by their tens of thousands on trains from Drancy to Auschwitz.

So I now had a third piece of landscape. I did another drawing, this time with three circles. One circle on the right hand side of the page, to show Turkey in the East, and one on the left side of the page, for France, and a third circle towards the middle of the page, slightly higher up, for Poland which is to the North-East of France. I now had three places.

And three dates: date of birth, date of convoy, date of death.

I didn't know what date he was arrested, when he was actually taken from his house somewhere in France and taken to Drancy, but I knew he was taken from Drancy on Convoy number 3 on the 22nd of June, and it was 22 days later, on the 14th of July, that he was murdered in Auschwitz.

21

The strategy of curiosity

You may be wondering why I was so curious about Ignace. I know I used to think, quite often, when Mrs. E. was asking me questions over and over, that she was taking her curiosity too far, and sometimes, I admit, it drove me mad.

But curiosity is useful. I remember her talking to me, when I was six, about why I had trouble talking in school. She was curious. She said, "Nobody really knows. I wonder… maybe it was because you had all those years of travelling when you were little, when you were talking only with your mom and dad, because all the people around you in those other countries didn't even speak your own language? And then suddenly you had to stay in one country and go to school and speak to people who were not your mom and dad. Maybe that was a bit scary? I wonder…"

One of Mrs. E.'s favourite strategies is using the phrase 'I wonder.' She used it often in those days, and she still does. Perhaps you could call it a *Strategy of Wondering*. Or maybe, *The Strategy of Curiosity*.

I have already told you that there is a lot Mrs. E. doesn't know, and then she gets this look in her eye, a kind of sideways and upwards look, and she puts her hand on her chin, and says "Hmm... I wonder, I'm curious, what if..." and then we get into these conversations, about all kinds of things, nothing to do with the things we are supposed to be working on.

So in that way she is very different from other teachers, because the only thing most teachers seem to be curious about is why I refuse to do homework, or why I have an Attitude.

Curiosity. It is something my dad has, for sure. Every time he goes onto a new site, exploring a new desert, he has to find out things he didn't know before, and if he wasn't curious he probably wouldn't find out anything. We talked about it a few times before his last trip, because he was telling us about someone on his team, and how that person was a world expert in methodology, how to do chemical tests on sand and how to send robots into the desert to collect samples, but what he lacked was curiosity. My dad was asking him questions and this colleague kept saying, "Wow, I never thought of that. We need to look into that!"

So I was also curious. I wanted to know more about Ignace. I went to the school library but they had very little on the Holocaust. The school librarian suggested I go to my local municipal library; they sent me to the Wiener Library for the Study of the Holocaust and Genocide.

It was through the Wiener Library that I unearthed more. The librarian there showed me four thick, heavy books, the work of two people, Serge and Beata Klarsfeld, who documented the actions of the Germans in

France during the war. The Klarsfelds were Nazi hunters and tried to find, and to bring to trial, people who were killers during the war and who had walked free afterwards, with no consequences for what they had done.

The Klarsfelds spent years tracking and collecting the documents on which the Nazis had listed every person arrested, every person taken to a detention camp, every person deported to a concentration camp, and every person murdered.

The thought of people making lists of their murder victims made me suddenly wonder whether my lists of words, and of fossil names, meant that perhaps I was actually as weird as my classmates think. But of course there is a huge difference: I don't actually murder people to get them onto my lists.

Serge Klarsfeld knew what he was doing when he started this work, because he had been a Jewish child in France at that time, and he too was at risk of being caught and murdered. His father was taken in 1943, and Serge and his mother and sister hid in a false partition in a cupboard to avoid arrest.

When the Nazis broke into the building and beat up their friends and neighbours, they could hear everything. They heard the screaming and the shouting for help. He and his mother and sister stayed hidden, they made not a sound, and were not found and not taken.

So Serge Klarsfeld knew something about silence. Their survival in that cupboard depended on their absolute silence. But after the war he broke his silence, and he started to tell the world about what the Nazis had done. The Klarsfelds spent years searching for documents detailing what had happened in those years, and they put together a list of every single Jew who had lived in France and had been deported or killed or sent to a camp during that war. The list is called 'Memorial to Jews Deported from France.'

They counted the names and it added up to 75,721 Jews. They realised that there may have been more; some names were lost, and some were spelled incorrectly.

Some were babies who didn't know or couldn't say their own names, so their names are not on the lists.

I thought about that number: 75,721. All those people, shouting their names from the lists.

On the Klarsfeld documents, each name is listed in a very organised way: first the surname, then the first name, then date of birth, place of birth, nationality, and the number and date of the train convoy which took them from France to the concentration camps.

I found that the lists are published online and you can search for a name through the Klarsfeld website. I scrolled down the list to the 'E's and I found his name. Edelstein, Ignace. There is also a photocopy of a typed document, now faded, so it is not easy to read; you have to look carefully. Just as I had read in the first list I had found, the one with the names of Sephardic Jews deported from France, there was his name, date of birth, place of birth, convoy number 3, and the date of the convoy's departure from France to Auschwitz. I suppose the other website had got their information from the Klarsfeld list.

But what was new for me in this Klarsfeld list was an address and a profession.

Address: 12 Impasse Briare, 9th Arondissement, Paris. Profession: jeweller.

I had to get up and walk away from the computer because it was too much, in one go, to find out. I couldn't take it all in. So few words, just an address and a profession, but suddenly he was a person, someone who had a house and a job and who went to work and went home and went to sleep and got up the next day to go to work again, making jewellery.

I stood by the window of the Wiener library for a few minutes and went back to the computer.

I had a thousand questions I would have wanted to ask. I looked at the list again. The font is very small, you have to keep looking, you have to get your eye in just like when you are looking for fossils, and you never know what you might find. I read his name over and over, trying to imagine him as a person and not as a name on a list.

Then I went back to the first list I had found and looked for other people with the same surname. There was another name, right above Ignace's name: Andre Edelstein. Also born in Constantinople.

Date of birth 24th April 1907; sent from Drancy, in Paris, to Auschwitz on Convoy number 46, 9th February 1943.

Surely this was Ignace's brother. Born in the same city. Four years younger than Ignace.

Back to the Klarsfeld lists for the address. The same address in Paris: Impasse Briare.

I was struck by such a shock, I couldn't breathe. It wasn't a Heart Attacker moment, it was something different. Something emerging, something changing, and it seemed like suddenly two real people had appeared, standing just there, near the window at the side of the Wiener library where a soft beam of sunlight falls diagonally. A man and his brother.

22

A story can happen when no-one is looking

I have been listening to stories since I can remember. My parents began reading to me when I was still a baby; my mother made up those little stories when she was teaching me to read; teachers were always reading storybooks to us in class. These days I mostly read detective stories: I am never without a book.

I suppose I have been imagining stories forever too; definitely before I started school, and even after I started school, when I was not speaking.

You don't need to speak to make up a good story.

And I did that in my speech therapy sessions too, in Mrs. E.'s room, when I was five. She had that tool box, the one with all the little dividers like my fossil boxes, with those lovely miniature toys. She would ask me which characters I wanted to play with during that session, and I would choose a few, maybe two animals and one doll.

I would also take out three or four props, perhaps some toy furniture, or a car or some pretend food, and I would start to play. I didn't tell the story with words; I just moved the pieces around and made up scenes and things that happened to the little dolls and animals. What Mrs. E. did was to watch my characters, and notice what they were doing, and then she would tell my story for me. She put into words what my characters did, and she described what happened to them.

So I didn't have to speak; she spoke for me, but it was my own story and she never tried to change anything in my story. She just said the words that I was thinking.

Then she would write my stories down in her foolscap notepads and she would pull the pages out and give them to me. Each page had two punched holes on the side so I could take them home to add them to a story folder, and I could read them any time I wanted to. I have them to this day, and one day, when my mom decides to publish her stories, maybe Mrs. E. and I will publish these stories too. But until then they are just little stories which helped Mrs. E. to know what my characters were doing in their lives, even though I couldn't tell her with words because I wasn't yet speaking to her.

So the information I was discovering about Ignace was starting to feel like a story, a story about two brothers. Except that I didn't have anything to put in the story besides two people's names, a few place names, and some dates.

I started working with the dates and counting: How many days Ignace had lived between his arrest and his death, how many months between his arrest and Andre's arrest; how many other people were on the convoy with him. The numbers and dates started going round and round in my head and I was spending hours with paper and pencil and a calculator, counting and calculating days and months.

Andre, if he was really the brother of Ignace, was deported to Auschwitz eight months after his brother. Only seven days before what would have been his brother's fortieth birthday, in February. But by then Ignace was dead.

Had they been able to communicate at all since the day that Ignace was arrested? How come Andre was not taken the same day that Ignace was, if they lived at the same address? Had Andre hidden? Was that why they didn't find him until nearly a year after they had taken Ignace?

Before he was taken, did Andre think he might be safe, that they had taken all the Jews they were going to take, that they had got enough dead Jews by now?

Another number: Andre was four years younger than his brother Ignace. Jasper is four and a half years younger than me.

I sat in the Wiener library for hours reading about Drancy, the camp where Jewish people were sent to await their transport to Auschwitz. I read about the horrific conditions there, the overcrowding, the sadistic guards, the filth and illness and the lack of food and medicine and the constant presence of death; the parents searching for their children because sometimes the Nazis took parents without their children, and sometimes they took children without their parents.

What had Ignace been thinking while he was there? He must have been desperately worried about his younger brother. And when Andre got to Drancy, eight months later, he must have known Ignace had been there. Did he search for him in the hope that he was still there? Andre must have felt a double loss now: to be where Ignace had last been, and not to find him there; and to know now for sure that he was gone, but not to know more. Because at that time the fate of those who were sent from Drancy by train was not yet known.

I read about those trains, jam-packed full of people, too many to leave space to sit down, no food or water or toilets. I imagined the trains starting to move slowly, then picking up speed, then the long, long trip, hour after hour, nobody knowing where they would end up and how they could survive this journey.

Things were suddenly moving too fast. I remembered the strategy Mrs. E. taught me to use if I felt that I wasn't comfortable in her session, if I felt scared or worried or if I couldn't breathe or if she was making the changes happen too fast, too many steps at a time. I just had to put up my hand, like a stop sign, and she would know I wasn't happy, and we would do something different; she might give me a different game to play with, or maybe go and make tea while I calmed down a bit.

I wished I could put up a hand and stop this happening to Ignace, maybe even stop the convoy, but it was going too fast.

There were other detention centres in France where Jews were held before being sent to concentration camps, but Drancy was the biggest. Altogether, 67,400 Jews were deported from Drancy during the war, in a total of 64 train transports.

Ignace's transport, convoy number 3, was made up of 1000 people; 933 men and 66 women. Of those, only 24 men and 5 women were alive after the war.

Andre's convoy, number 46, also had 1000 people. How meticulous those Nazis were, making sure that everything was so precise, so exact. Precisely 1000 people per convoy.

Looking at Andre's convoy details in the Klarsfeld list I found a new category, which had not been there in 1942 when Ignace was taken: "Gassed on arrival."

From Andre's convoy, 77 men and 92 women were selected to work at Auschwitz. The rest, 816 people, were gassed on arrival. After the war, 21 men and 7 women were alive from Andre's convoy.

There were also children on those convoys: 11,400 children in total. I found another list, also compiled by Serge Klarsfeld, titled 'French Children of the Holocaust: A Memorial.' This book includes photographs – not that many photographs survived the displacement and imprisonment in concentration camps – but the Klarsfelds carefully collected what they could and published them in the book, along with the list of names.

I saw that in the first convoys very few children were included; that came later. There was only one child on Convoy number 3, on the train with Ignace. Jacques Bronfman, age 17.

Somebody's child. A teenager like me. A boy like Jasper.

I started to understand how a real guardian, a responsible Guardian of Memory might feel: you start to live with that person, you find your life connected with his in strange ways, and you wonder what you will discover next, and the more you find out the worse the news gets and the more horrific the story and your heart is beating as fast as a Heart Attacker but you know you can't stop looking now.

That's when the hopelessness of responsibility started to become clear to me.

In the meantime my life was going on as usual at school and at home. Jasper was still irritating me and I was still irritating some of my teachers. And all my spare time was now spent online, searching for Ignace.

I hadn't told my parents; they thought that my visits to the Wiener library were for some school project. I didn't know how to tell them, and I also thought, maybe there is nothing to tell yet, I have found out so little.

But one day, when I was at Mrs. E. working on a paper I had to write, because even though I had done a successful oral presentation and there were no new complaints about me from the teachers, my parents thought I should keep seeing her until the end of that school term, I decided to tell her.

When I told Mrs. E. what I was doing, and what I had found out, she was quiet for a while. I thought perhaps she wasn't pleased I was doing all this searching; after all she was the real, the official Guardian of his Memory; she had the certificate and she had the right to do it herself. I hoped she wouldn't feel that I had hijacked her certificate or stepped on her toes somehow.

But what she said, after she had been quiet for a while, was that however old she is, she is always learning something new, and what she learned that day was that some people of thirteen are ten times as wise as people of sixty-three.

She said that if I needed help with this project she would be happy to help me, but that I must guide her;

I must tell her if I needed her to join in the search and what I wanted her to search for, because I was now in charge. And even if I didn't need any help, she said she would be 'most grateful' if I told her what I found out, because that way we could both be the guardians of the memory of Ignace Edelstein, and the more we knew about him the better we could remember him.

23

Changes

I wasn't doing homework, I wasn't working on my notebooks or my dictionary, and I wasn't sleeping well.

I was searching.

I started to think about where the brothers had lived when they were caught. The address said it was in the 9th Arondissement in Paris. I looked at online maps of Paris and found out that Paris is divided into areas, called Arondissements. The 9th has some wide streets, some big department stores, some museums and galleries and the beautiful old Opera House.

I enlarged the online maps and I found the street. Then I looked on Google Street View and saw it as it is today, as it would look if you were there, standing in the street.

The place where Ignace lived is not an actual street but a narrow alley, a passageway, between two rows of big buildings with beautiful wrought iron balconies. If you look on Google Street View you can see the shops at street level: a travel agency on one side of the alleyway and an art gallery or maybe a framer on the other side of the alleyway. I think the buildings might have been really grand and expensive once, but it doesn't look like a very posh street now, just an ordinary street with

shops downstairs and flats above and quite a lot of
traffic going by. In the Street View photograph the
narrow entrance to the alleyway is half obscured by a
traffic light; I wished the person taking the pictures for
Street View had managed to avoid it, because it was
blocking my view.

I trawled through the internet for hours and found,
published online, a very old photograph, in black and
white, or maybe it is sepia, taken of that passage. The
photograph was taken in the early days of photography,
in 1860, and it was clearly the same place I could see on
Street View. I printed it and framed it; it is sitting on my
desk now as I write.

In another place on the Klarsfeld website I found a
copy of Ignace's death certificate. The Nazis were so
efficient: they wrote everything down, and kept every
piece of evidence of their deeds. Not even an attempt
to hide it or to cover it up.

This is a copy of the exact words, from the Nazi death
certificate, written in Auschwitz, for Ignace:

'Edelstein, Ignace (1903-02-16 1942-07-14)

*Birthplace: Konstantinopel, Residence: Paris IX,
Religion: Jew.'*

And that was it. Those were all the facts I could find.

I wanted to know why he had moved, why he had gone
from Turkey to Paris, why he had made that fateful
change which led to his death.

I know something about change of place. Not just because my family has done so much travelling, and not just because of changing schools, but also because of something else I suddenly remembered.

Back when I was six years old, after about a year of therapy in Mrs. E.'s house, she told me we would soon stop having our sessions at her office; instead she would have a room at the school and I would see her there. She told me we would have the same toys, the box with the miniatures and the tree house, and we would have our own room, but it would be at the school.

That was a big change for me. Much bigger than that day when she had come to visit my classroom and had sat there quietly saying nothing.

I was not happy with that, not at all. I didn't want any changes. I didn't want to be at school anyway, and I definitely didn't want Mrs. E. to become one of the school teachers. But it was not up to me, and a month later she had a new room at the school. It was a tiny room, which used to be where they kept the overflow books which didn't fit in the library, so it was not nearly as nice as the room she had in her own house.

Also there was a strange smell there, a kind of damp smell. I suppose that was because we were in the basement. I hated that room and it took me a long time to stop being cross with Mrs. E. about the room. I checked to see if she had really brought all the games, our favourites, and the tree house, and sure enough she had, but it felt so strange, and it smelled so ugly, and I didn't feel like talking there at all. The worst thing about it was, I never knew who would walk past or even walk right into the room while I was there.

And I thought that Mrs. E. should not have let that change happen.

Mrs. E. asked me to help her decorate the new room, because it had no pictures on the walls, and the cupboards were a big mess, with all her toys just dumped inside. So together we decided how to arrange the room, and she bought stacking boxes and I made labels with her label maker so that we could organise all the stationery and the coloured paper and the games. Slowly the room started to look more like a room I would want to be in, and she bought some pictures to hang up on the walls and it felt a bit more like home after that.

We carried on with our usual activities in the new room: playing word games, and making up stories with the characters from the tool box, and Mrs. E. carried on writing down my stories for me, which by that time I was able to tell her, because I had made so much progress in speech therapy. And gradually I forgave her for moving to the basement room in the school, although I never did get used to the smell, and one day when we played a game called 'I wish', what I said for my wish was that I wished we could go back to being in her old room, and walk through the stained glass colours of the entrance hall into her room which smelled like wild honeysuckle.

Now that I am older, I can see that she probably got me to help her decorate the room so that I would feel more familiar with it, so that I would feel I had some responsibility for that space, and perhaps I wouldn't feel the effects of the change as so hurtful.

I wondered how Ignace managed his change, from Turkey in the East to Paris in the West; whether he found the change easy, and whether he later thought about the terrible consequences of the change he had made.

24

Tracking

I had nothing else I wanted to think about or write about, so I carried on handing in papers with the same title. My English teacher didn't seem to mind; in fact she was becoming more and more interested in how my search was going, and asked if I would be willing to talk about this to the class, on Holocaust Memorial Day, but I refused. Politely.

Searching for Ignace Edelstein (Part 2)

By Amethyst Simons

I have been searching for a person. A person who is dead.

I only know a few real facts about this person: his name, his date of birth, and the day he was murdered. I also know what his job was, and I know his address, the place where he was living in Paris on the day he was arrested by the French police and sent to Auschwitz.

The little information I have is really nothing more than some faint fossilized scratchings on a piece of sandstone, like the marks left by a wave moving over sand, or the tracks made by the feet and tail of a trilobite walking across a beach millions of years ago. They are not the whole person or the real person, but the faintest trail left behind by him.

But these few facts are all I have to work with. I am trying to be a detective, and from these few facts I am trying to re-create not just a story, not just a biography, but a whole life. The life of Ignace Edelstein.

Michelangelo worked from the outside in: He took a huge block of granite and hewed away until he revealed the person within. I have to do the opposite: I have to work from the inside out. I have a few facts about the person and I have to build up, not hew down. I have to build and add and flesh out. I have to put those facts in a place and a time and a landscape, until I have a complete person.

In science you start with a hypothesis and try it out; you test it to see if it holds. If you can find something to disprove it you have learned that your hypothesis needs to be adjusted. But you have to start with a hypothesis.

This is how detectives work, and this is how archaeologists work: they look at a few clues, and they fill in the gaps; they hypothesize a story. Sometimes they see tracks or lines on a field, which become clear perhaps only at sunset when the sun's angle falls just so onto the field, and knowing the history of the area they hypothesize what might be found there, and they dig a trench to see if their hypothesis was correct.

Here's an example. From the pattern of wear on the teeth of stone age skeletons you can make a guess, you can infer, that these people ate roots and bulbs, not just meat, and this helps you guess that they would have used some kind of digging tool or stick to dig up the roots and bulbs. The fact that all you find in that site is arrowheads does not mean that all they ate was meat that they had hunted; even though you don't find a single digging stick it is not because they didn't use them, but because wood does not last over thousands of years; it decays.

So you may find no actual facts about what happened long ago; all you have is hints and guesses, but you can still make inferences and build up a hypothesis.

I have often said that words are important, and this was another example of how that is true. Finding that word, the word "jeweller", in the list with Ignace's name and address, made it possible for me to see Ignace more clearly. I was able to build up a hypothesis and to know so much more about him because of that one word.

So even though I have no way of knowing for sure that Ignace was a perfectionist like me, I can make an inference from the fact that he was a jeweller; a jeweller living in Paris at a time when Paris was the centre of art and creativity and design. I know this because I did some research about life in Paris in the 1930's and the 1940's. There is no way Ignace would have been able to make a living as a jeweller in Paris at that time, to have 'jeweller' listed on the Nazi deportation lists as his profession, without his having been extremely good at his work; in fact, a perfectionist.

That is how I know things about him. I am a tracker. I am trying to do the same kind of thing that a tracker in the Kalahari does when he is hunting for food. They follow the clues and make a hypothesis, and set off to see if it is correct, and then they can put together a story about the animal they are tracking.

Of course you can make a mistake and make a wrong assumption. Once when thousands of animal bones were found at a prehistoric site in Spain, people assumed that this had been the 'dining room' of a group of hunters who had hunted and killed all these animals. But it is just as possible that this place with all its skeletons of animals could have been a marsh, where animals gathered to drink, and over many, many years some of them died there. The marsh would have preserved their bones, over thousands of years. So you have to be careful when making inferences because it can lead you totally on the wrong track.

So here is my hypothesis, the story I think is the real thing, about Ignace. I don't know if it is correct. Perhaps I have mis-read the clues in the landscape, and perhaps I have made inferences which are not true. I hope he will forgive me if that is the case.

Ignace Edelstein was born in Constantinople, which is now called Istanbul, in Turkey. He had a brother, Andre, who was four years younger. His parents were Abraham and Fany Edelstein.

In Turkey in those days, Jews lived relatively safely, and there was very little persecution and very little danger. But there were other problems; people were being forcibly conscripted into the army, and there were economic difficulties. The news from Europe and America was all about the many young people who had left Turkey and gone overseas and had found a good life, and how they were making their fortunes there.

Lots of young people from the Jewish community were leaving; some went to Europe, and many to America. Ignace dreamed about going to a new place. But the thing that really got him thinking seriously about leaving was a string of violent attacks against Jews in

1934, in an area called Thrace which is now part of Bulgaria but at that time belonged to Turkey.

That year, the Turkish government had passed a new law which aimed to make minorities integrate more into Turkish society; it was called a Resettlement Law, and included forcing people to move from one area to another, so that minorities would not be living in large groups together.

The law led to unrest all over Turkey. It is unbelievable that while all minorities were affected by this new law, it was the Jews who were scapegoated. In Thrace, Jewish shops and houses were vandalized and people were physically attacked; thousands fled from the region and came to Constantinople, where they told their stories to people they met there. So Ignace knew very well what can happen when people turn on minorities and attack them.

But it wasn't only getting away from danger that made him want to move. It was the whole idea of Paris: the art and culture and glamour. And something was pushing him to make a decision soon: there was news of an international exhibition to be held in May 1937, an exhibition of art and design, in Paris.

Paris had, since 1900, become the centre of new creative ideas in the arts, with people like Picasso, Chagall, Matisse and Modigliani working there. Artists from all over the world were moving to live and work in Paris, and Ignace wanted to be there too.

Ignace was a jeweller and he wanted to see what was being done in art and design in Paris. As a jeweller he felt stuck in an Eastern tradition, and he was thirsty for any news from Paris about the latest, most modern fashion and design and jewellery. He spent hours looking at magazines with photographs and illustrations, but it was not enough, because he had no real contact with the people actually working in France at the time.

It would be relatively easy for him to go to France, because all educated Turks spoke French. In Constantinople there was a French Jewish school and many Jews were completely fluent in the language. Several women students were going to Paris to train as teachers. Young men were leaving Turkey and going to Paris for adventure, glamour, and work.

Ignace and Andre may not have been rich, but what they both had was a profession: Ignace was a jeweller, and Andre was a radio technician. And that meant they could go anywhere and find work. Ignace and his brother were young, they were adventurous, they were single, they wanted to see the world, and Paris was the most exciting place they could think of.

One evening, when they were sitting at their parents' dinner table on Friday night, after their mother had lit the Sabbath candles and they had eaten their meal, and they were talking about all kinds of things, they got on to the subject of Ignace's feelings about Turkey and he told them of his decision to try his luck in Paris, for a year or two, and see how he liked it.

Andre had always followed his older brother's lead, and announced there and then that he was determined to go too.

In a way, Ignace was sorry his brother was coming with him, because he felt a little guilty at leaving his aging parents behind. But he had always felt a sense of responsibility to Andre, because Andre was so much younger and had always needed to be protected by his older brother.

So they wrote to some friends who had left for Paris a few years before and were now familiar with the place, and asked them to find them a small flat, somewhere central, to rent. The flat which was found for them was in the 9th Arondissement, at number 12, Impasse Briare, which suited Ignace perfectly, because it was not far from the area where the artists were living and working and meeting each other: Montmartre.

So it was that Ignace made a big change in his life: he moved from East to West, from living with his parents to living more independently, from always looking elsewhere for new ideas and inspiration, to having it right there on his doorstep.

I think change must have been long overdue for Ignace, and I think he must have loved his time in Paris.

In some ways, I am a person who hates change. I hated going to a new school and I hated moving to a new house. But on the other hand, my parents have been taking me to other countries and other cities since I was small, and I have never felt stuck in a place, wishing I could see more of the world.

So maybe what I hate about change is not the change of place, but having to deal with new people, to talk to new people. I actually like changing places, seeing new things, and doing different things, and learning something that I never knew before. So I can imagine how Ignace felt when he made his change; the excitement of exploring a new place.

Maybe 'change' is not something you can like or dislike in itself. A teacher once asked me if I don't like change. You can't answer a question like that; it has to be a specific question. What kind of change do you like? What kind of change do you hate?

For me the answer to those questions is actually nothing to do with change: it is, how do you like spending your time? With people? Or with your own thoughts? Talking or writing? Seeing new things? Finding new places? And once you have answered how you like to spend your time, then it becomes obvious whether you like change or not.

I don't know the year when Ignace moved from Turkey to France, or how old he was, and I don't know how many years he had in his dream city, Paris, before he was murdered. But I hope that he had a few happy years to live with the change he had made and I hope he found what he was looking for.

He sits at his work table, the leather apron covering his lap to protect him from the heat of the soldering, the apron with the cuff to catch any gold particles that may fall off the table.

He starts up the small pendant drill; he readies his soldering torch, he puts on his protective goggles. He has to be careful of his eyes, but also of his hands: any injury to his hands or eyes would mean the end of his career, the end of who he is. He is a jeweller. His work is in his hands and his eyes and his imagination. His head is bowed in total concentration. This is not team work; this is one person doing one thing, and doing it perfectly. To talk to him now would be to distract him, to cause him to make a mistake, to bend the metal before it is ready to be bent, to chip a precious stone, to drop something.

My parents were worried about me; they said I was getting morbid, because I couldn't stop thinking about Ignace, and reading about Drancy and Auschwitz.

They were right, I was getting morbid and I couldn't stop. I had to find him. Even if it was almost impossible, even if he was buried like a fossil under tons of rock for millions of years and there were almost no clues to help me find him.

I do know something about searching, I do sometimes find fossils, and I was going to find Ignace.

25

The museum

As soon as we came back from my thirteenth birthday trip I started to plan my next birthday trip, for my fourteenth. I know it seems stupid to plan the next one right after the current one, but I didn't really need to think much; it was obvious to the whole family what I would choose. I wanted to go to France.

There is a museum in Paris, a memorial to the Holocaust, where they have put up a huge granite wall, called the Wall of Names. On it are engraved the names of all those Jews who were deported to concentration camps by the Nazis. I wanted to see what a wall of 70,000 names looks like, how big it must be to take all those names, and what kind of granite they have used. But most of all I wanted to be sure that Ignace and his brother really had a place on that wall.

At that museum they also keep documents, like those collected by the Klarsfelds, and I wanted to go there to try to find more information.

Except this time, we had a problem. My dad was not working. The university he worked for was in financial trouble and they were offering redundancy to people, even people who had worked for them for a really long time. So now my dad was trying to set up his own business as a geology adviser to some mining companies, and in the meantime, while he was not working, we needed to be careful with money.

My mother had an idea. She said, "Since you are already thirteen, you can start earning money in holiday jobs."

I thought that was a good idea, but there was another problem about going to France: the language. Nobody in our family knows French very well; my dad can speak a bit but is not good at reading French. I needed someone who could not only ask the way, but who could read and translate for me the documents in the museum. And the only person I could think of, who I knew spoke French, and the only person I would trust with this job, was Ignace's other guardian, Mrs. E.

Which meant I had to earn not only enough money for my ticket (my mom said she would pay for her ticket, and this time, my dad and Jasper would stay home to save money) but I also had to pay for Mrs. E.'s ticket, because I was not going to ask her to pay a huge amount of money for something that was really my birthday present.

My dad said it was a good lesson in waiting, because we all knew it would take a long time to make enough money at a holiday job. I was actually quite upset, not that I thought I shouldn't have a holiday job, but because it was the first time in our family that a birthday trip was in doubt. And also because it was still a while before the summer holidays, when I would be able to start a job, and all that time I wasn't finding anything new about Ignace, and I was stuck with the little I knew.

My mom was still worried that I was obsessing too much about finding Ignace. She said to me, "What if you get to Paris, and we go to the documentation centre, and you still can't find anything more about him?" But I thought, if I could even just see his name on the wall, that would be something.

So my dad spoke to someone at the Museum of London, and though they have a policy of not taking volunteers who are under eighteen, he knew people there and they agreed to interview me and they said that if they found me suitable they would give me a chance. My dad told me what they said: they needed people who were 'serious', and 'mature' – that is no problem for me, I can say that much about myself – but they also mentioned the words 'good social skills' and 'someone who can take groups of school children around and explain the exhibits to them' and I thought, well that's it, they will never take me.

Because even though I am not a selective mute any more, I know I don't have good social skills, and maybe I have no social skills at all, good or otherwise. I don't like talking to people I don't know, I don't like small talk, I don't chat. Some girls in my class call me weird and they are probably right.

As usual when there are problems with me, my parents spoke first to my grandmother and then they spoke to Mrs. E.

My grandmother said, "Nonsense! Amethyst is the most sensible and capable person I know, I would hire her any time!" but Mrs. E. was a bit more cautious, and she asked for a day or two to think about it.

When I next went to a session with her she said, "Let's talk this through. What duties do you think they may ask you to do in this job?"

All I knew was what they had told my dad. So we looked online and saw that they were offering guided tours for teachers, where a teacher can bring a class, or a small group of kids, to the museum, and a guide would take them around and explain things.

Mrs. E. wasted no time. She got my mom to phone my English teacher and offer to host five kids in the class, as a reward perhaps for doing some good work on a project, by taking them on a tour of the museum which would be led by a guide who works there. So even though it made me cringe because it is definitely not cool to have your mother come to the class and talk to the kids, her idea was brilliant, because the five kids chosen (and I made sure that I would be one of them) got to take time off from school one morning and to have a guided tour at the museum.

Mrs. E. came with us, and all through the tour she and I were taking notes: not about the exhibits, which I had already seen a few times because I like to spend time at that museum, but about what the guide did: how she spoke, what she said, how she got the kids to move on from one place to the next, and to stop using their phones during the tour.

At my next session with Mrs. E. we compared notes. She had noticed a lot of things which I hadn't even thought of: how the guide greeted us at the door, what she said when she was introducing the tour and how she explained the rules about behaviour and about sticking together.

Mrs. E. also noticed how the guide made her voice just loud enough so that all the kids would hear her, but not so loud as to disturb other people visiting the museum. She had made notes about how the guide ended the tour: she had noticed how she got us to go via the shop before leaving so we would be sure to spend some money, which the museum probably needs for their running costs.

So we went over and over the list and role-played it until I was reasonably sure I would be able to handle a tour like that.

Mrs. E. also coached me in interview techniques. Always walk into the room with your head straight up, don't tilt it to the side, it makes you look unsure of yourself. Always make sure to look the interviewer in the eye, because they like eye contact, even if you hate it. (She knew me very well by then, having worked with me in my selective mutism days.) Make sure to look at all the interviewers, if there are more than one, so nobody feels left out, because the one you leave out will not like you and will feel you are not up to the job.

Mrs. E. made me walk into the room and greet her, over and over, because she said the first few moments of an interview can be the deciding factor. She made me practice a confident handshake and greeting, over and over, until she was satisfied that I looked sufficiently mature and confident.

By the time the day of the interview arrived I was sick of the whole thing, but I knew that if I ever have to be interviewed for a university application or a job, or if I ever have to give a talk in public, I will know all the strategies. Not 'small steps' this time, but *Strategies for Confident Talking*.

Well you can imagine what a good interview I had, because besides talking to the interviewers about my fossil collection and my interest in landscape archaeology,

I could also tell them that I felt competent in guiding a tour, because I had made a study of tour management and I could give them very practical examples of what I meant.

This was not the first time Mrs. E. has shown me that having a strategy can get you what you want in life, and I hope it won't be the last time, because having a strategy is what made it possible for me to earn some money, and to go to Paris with my mom and Mrs. E.

I started working at the museum on the first day of the July school holidays. A funny thing happened when I was working there. I wasn't the only guide; there were three others, all older than me. They had all finished school and were having a gap year or waiting for the university term to start.

We had to share out the work between us. I didn't want to take the teenage groups because I am a teenager myself and I didn't think the kids would listen to me, so the older volunteers agreed to do those, and I was happy to do the younger kids' tours, because I just imagined myself dealing with irritating kids like my brother Jasper, and I knew exactly how to handle them.

That's not the funny thing I want to tell you. The funny thing was that the three other guides and I became a team. We helped each other out, we shared jokes about some of the awful kids who came on our tours, and some of the more awful teachers who brought them, and I remembered how one of the main complaints of my P.E. teacher was that I was not a team player. That's the funny thing I wanted to tell you about.

26

The voice of the xenolith

The summer holidays were coming to an end. I had saved up some money for the tickets by working every day and every weekend, but it was not enough. But everyone was suddenly very encouraging and interested in my project about finding Ignace, and my grandmother offered to lend us money so that we would have enough for our trip.

I was still seeing Mrs. E. once a week even though it was school holidays. At one of our sessions, after we had done some work on vocabulary and style, I told her about my new list of words: *'pro'* words. The main ones on this list were *protest* and *protect*.

I wanted to put the two words together, because I was sick of my parents and teachers worrying about me and it felt like they were suffocating me and over-protecting me, so I wanted to *protest against protection*.

She kind of understood what I was saying. She asked me to imagine something: If Silence is in charge on one side, and on the other side parents and teachers are also trying to take charge, because they are worried about you, how does it feel? When there are these forces on both sides of you, what is it like to sit between these two sides?

I thought that I didn't want to be caught like that. It felt suffocating, like I was caught between two big boulders.

But that made me suddenly think of my being a xenolith, a rock caught inside a rock of a completely different kind. And it was strange, because I have always loved the idea of being a xenolith, but now suddenly I thought that maybe the stone inside the rock is not there by choice but has been caught, and it can't get away, and maybe it feels suffocated.

I got a bit upset then, in fact I just wanted to cry, because all this time I had been thinking what a good thing it was to be a xenolith, how special it made me, and that idea really kept me going through all the mean comments from other girls in my class, and the trouble I was in with my teachers. And now I could see that maybe being a xenolith was the opposite of what I really wanted. I wanted to be free; free of all those people telling me how I should be, free of school and the teachers and the other kids in the class telling me I was weird to go on fossil-hunting holidays.

I wanted to get out of that rock that was holding me and not letting me go and was suffocating me.

I know that feeling of being suffocated: you can't breathe, your parents think you have asthma, and it is the Heart Attacker all over again.

I thought now that maybe I had been wrong all along about Michelangelo's Slave statues, and that unfinished obelisk in the quarry at Aswan. Maybe they were tragedies of unfinished work. Maybe Michelangelo had wanted to complete the statues and could not work out how to get them to emerge from the stone undamaged; maybe the quarry workers were devastated, or even punished, for allowing the obelisk to crack while they were excavating it. Maybe these works are suffocating inside their rock, never to emerge.

Mrs. E. could see I was upset. She waited a bit and then said something about how she was sorry she had upset me. So I had to tell her. I told her what a xenolith is (she had never heard that word; I suppose only a person who has a geologist in her family would ever know a word like that) and how the stone inside the rock is a singular thing on its own, and how I saw that as the way I am, different from the people who are around me, surrounded by something other than myself. We looked at pictures of xenoliths online so she could see what a xenolith looks like. I told her the Greek origin of the word and I could see she was interested.

"It seems to me," she said, "that you are right about that. It is a good metaphor to use for a person who is not like everyone else, who has original ideas, who can think for herself. But could it be, is it possible, that in the same way that we found the meaning of granite to have more than one way it can be used as a metaphor for people, this word, the xenolith, also has some different possibilities? Not instead of that meaning, but in addition to that meaning?"

I couldn't think of anything except how dumb I had been, pretending to be something special all this time when actually I was just weird, odd, a misfit, just like some people in my class had been saying.

It reminded me of a game I used to play with Mrs. E. when I was still going to her for speech therapy because I was a selective mute. It was called 'Odd One Out.' The game is made up of lots of small cards; each card has four pictures on it. Three of the four pictures would be pictures of things that belong in one group, for example three kinds of fruit, and one of the pictures on the card would be something from a completely different category, for example a type of clothing, perhaps a shirt, or socks. What we had to do, in turn, was to pick a card, and say which picture of the four didn't fit into the group, and explain why it didn't fit.

Most of the cards were quite easy, even for a five-year-old, like the fruit and clothes, but some were a bit harder; one card had three things you wear in winter (a coat, a scarf and boots) and the fourth picture, the odd one out, was a T-shirt which is something you wear in summer.

There was one card I especially liked, because it had only flowers on it, so at first it seemed that all four pictures belonged to the same group, and there was no odd one out, but when you looked carefully you saw that one of the flowers, the rose, was the only flower with thorns.

I suppose I was good at that game because I was the odd one out: the xenolith, the one who is different from the others. Who doesn't fit into any group.

But in those days, when we used to play 'Odd One Out,' I didn't feel left out, or weird. It was actually fun. Mrs. E. and I would take turns, so that it wasn't me doing all the talking. And Mrs. E. would make little jokes. At the beginning, when I first started to go to speech therapy, we never had jokes and nothing was very funny. But later she started to make jokes; she would act silly, as if she didn't know the answer to a question. In this game she liked to pretend that she couldn't see which one was the odd one out, and she would give me all kinds of silly reasons why something didn't fit into the group.

So when we looked at the card with the flowers, which I knew, having looked at it carefully for a while, was about the one flower which had thorns, she thought for a while and then she looked at me and I could just see she was going to make a joke. I know that face that grown-ups make: it is a kind of upside-down smile, where they make the corners of their lips go down instead of up but their eyes are crinkling with a smile anyway. She pointed to the picture of the daisy, and said, "That's the odd one out, because a daisy is cold, and the others are flowers which are hot."

She knew as well as I did that it was nonsense, but she looked so funny with her silly smile, that I didn't mind speaking, and I said to her, "No, it's the rose, because a rose has thorns."

I think that was the first time I managed to say a whole sentence in front of Mrs. E., all those words, without even noticing at the time that I had done it and without noticing that I had felt no fear.

When I think of that sentence, it was probably also the first time I had disagreed with an adult who was not someone in my family. So I think that was a big step for me in my *bravery strategies*. Saying something that was different, not what was expected, something that would make someone sit up and listen. When all I had always really wanted was *not* to be listened to.

I suppose, looking back on that day now, that it was those games we played which helped me to learn how to use my voice and to speak to people who were not my family. But it wasn't just the games, because those games were really simple, and we played them at home too. It was Mrs. E., how she let me trust her and how she smiled with the crinkles next to her eyes. Most of all it was how she knew when to speak and when to be silent, and not to push me to do anything that would stop my breathing. How she never let me feel like I was the Odd One Out when I was with her. How she used the strategy of small steps to take me very, very slowly, out of the land of the Heart Attacker into a new landscape where people could talk if they felt like it. And how she used her own silence to help me feel comfortable with silence.

And now here we were again, years later, still talking about Silence.

"I wonder…" said Mrs. E., "I wonder if perhaps I made a mistake when I thought that Silence comes back to mess things up for you. I think I was wrong, because now I think, could it be that Silence comes along as a helper?"

She was doing it again, talking about Silence like it was a live thing, something that comes along and does things.

She went on, "It seems to me that maybe Silence helps you to protect your ideas, to keep them from getting messed up, or mixed up, to keep them perfect. Could it be that the way Silence helps you to protect your ideas is the same as the way the rock protects the xenolith inside it?"

I thought about the things I protect. My notebooks with all my ideas, and my dictionary with its different groups of words, and my fossils categorised and labelled in my tool boxes. All the things and the ideas that are precious to me are kept in their places, protected in my room at home, organised, arranged, perfect. Nobody in my family touches my stuff or rearranges it or even dusts it; I look after it myself.

I am like a curator of a museum, protecting my finds. I look after my books and my fossils and my ideas, the things I know. All those things that other kids don't know, about other countries and languages and about geology and sand: I protect my thoughts and my ideas.

I said nothing. I was thinking.

Mrs. E. was silent too, for a long time. Then she said, "Maybe in the classroom, Silence comes along when you need a helper, when you need to protect your ideas, to keep them clear and perfect by keeping them to yourself, by not diluting them with explanations and trying to get people to listen. But when you needed to protect your parents and help them to find Jasper, Silence knew that it wasn't needed at that time, that something else was needed, so did it bow out at that time? Or did you feel that you would rather be silent when that thing was happening?"

Well obviously, I didn't stay silent that time, I shouted until someone listened to me. Mrs. E. kept going. "Do you remember we talked about how you use your strength to protect things? To protect your fossils, and your ideas, and your brother? Can you see how these things are linked?"

I couldn't see what she was on about. I was not getting my eye in, I didn't know what she was talking about, and everything just seemed wrong to me. I just wanted to go home.

She went on. "It seems to me that these things are linked. What if the rock around the stone, which is holding that stone tight, is trying to protect it, not to suffocate it? I wonder if that rock has protected the xenolith from being crushed by other rocks, from being weathered, from being picked up and taken by a collector? Perhaps they have a relationship of protection?"

"Well if that is the case, it is over-protection," I said. "Because the stone can't ever get away, the rock is stronger than the stone."

She sat, silent. I also had nothing to say so I sat and thought about all this stuff about rocks, and holding, and suffocating.

And then I got it. It wasn't one thing or the other; it was a bit of both. With a real xenolith, that stone is forever trapped inside the rock. But for me, well, I may be different from all the other kids, I may be the Odd One Out, but actually I can get out of my rock: I can do it whenever I want to. I can go travelling; I can get a holiday job and earn money; I can give a talk in front of the whole class.

And when I want to, I can get back into the shelter of my rock and be safe. I will still be different from other people, I will still be the amethyst in that rock, and what is precious to me will still be protected: my ideas and my interests.

She said, "I wonder if your name, Amethyst, is something to think about, because it is a word for a precious stone, and a precious stone reflects light. Or maybe it lets light shine through it. So even if it is inside a rock, even if it is a xenolith, it shines out of the rock."

I didn't know what she was talking about and I couldn't think straight by then, but luckily it was time to go home, because the session was over.

27

Numbers

I wrote this paper for the English teacher just before the end of the school year, in July.

<u>*Learning to count*</u>

<u>*By Amethyst Simons*</u>

The number of Jews deported from France to concentration camps, from the first roundup in May 1941 until the last one in August 1944, was 75,721. That is the number in the Klarsfeld lists, although some history books say it was more like 76,000. And of all those deported, only about 2,500 were alive after the war. So about 73,221 Jews from France were killed.

When the Germans invaded France, in 1940, there were about 300,000 Jews living in France.

That means about 25% of all the Jews living in France at the time were murdered. About a quarter.

I am trying to understand what the numbers mean, because numbers that big don't mean anything. You can't picture them, you can't imagine them or understand them.

Perhaps I can try to find an analogy.

'Analogy': a word derived from the Greek 'analogia' which means proportions, or ratio. Made up of two words: 'ana' which means upon, or according to, and 'logos' which means word, or speech, or reckoning.

So here is one kind of analogy. The London borough of Southwark has 288,700 people. That is nearly 300,000. Imagine if a quarter of those people were murdered.

I don't think I can picture it.

Maybe I can change the landscape, and instead of using a suburb of a huge city as an analogy, I can use a smaller city.

Take Brighton, for example. Now called Brighton and Hove, population 273,000 people. Look at the Ordnance Survey map, 1:25000 scale, where you can see the actual buildings in the town, drawn onto the map; then divide the town into four segments and cover up all of the houses in one of those segments using a permanent black marker. That's what happens when you murder one quarter of a population.

Maybe it is easier to grasp if I look at a town which has a population of the same number as the number of Jews who were murdered. For example, Weymouth and its neighbouring area, Portland. We have had seaside holidays in Weymouth, and of course my dad couldn't resist analysing the sand there because it is a beach with unusually fine sand; the size of each sand grain is one of the smallest in the whole of the UK. They have sandcastle building competitions there, and sand sculpture festivals, because the sand is so fine that it sticks together and makes it easier to build sandcastles. And we have visited Portland to look at the quarries where Portland stone is found, because my dad thought it would be an educational *trip for me and Jasper. Portland stone is a limestone and is still being quarried there; it was used in St Paul's Cathedral as well as Buckingham Palace.*

Weymouth and Portland. Population, 65,100.

Kill them all.

Here is another analogy: the street where you live. A quarter of all people means that out of all the people who live in your street, every fourth person would be taken away and murdered.

Or take your own house, that's a good analogy. Take a family like mine, my mom and dad and me and Jasper. One of us would be murdered.

There is actually no way to know what a number like 73,221 means. It is too big for our minds to manage. So maybe it makes it possible to imagine all those deaths if we just think of the two of them, Ignace and Andre, two brothers who came to France to find a better life and who died the worst death you can imagine

I originally planned to go to France for my fourteenth birthday, but I just couldn't wait that long. I was almost burning with the need to find out more about Ignace and to find out soon.

It took a lot of negotiation with my parents to let me have my birthday trip in advance, in fact nine months before the actual birthday, but I did it, and we, my mom and Mrs. E. and I, went in the last week of the school holidays.

We took the Eurostar to Paris and then the Metro from Gare du Nord and got off at Cadet Station. This must have been the Metro station which the police closed off when they were doing the arrests that night in June 1942, so that even if someone did manage to run away he would not be able to go far.

We walked down the big road with all the shops which I had seen on Google Street View: Rue de Maubege. It was quite a long walk and at first I thought we had made a mistake and come to the wrong place. But then I saw the travel agent's shop sign, and the art gallery, and between the two, the little opening to the alleyway.

I peered down the alley; I was scared to walk in, just in case someone was there and they saw us. I somehow needed this moment to be all on my own. To be quiet, unheard and unseen.

Mrs. E. and my mother were being sensitive. I knew this because I overheard them talking about it on the way, while we were still looking at the maps and finding the street. So they were hanging well back, because they knew how important it was for me to be there on my own, to be the first person to go where Ignace had been, knowing what I knew.

The alley looked strangely inviting; not at all how I had pictured it. I had imagined it as desolate or ruined, a place of war and fear, but on this sunny day in 2014 I saw beautiful antique street lamps, and pink and red geraniums blossoming in pots on windowsills, behind decorative wrought-iron window grilles. The houses were neatly painted and the street was spotlessly clean. In the sunshine on the day I was there, it looked such a pleasant place, such a happy place.

I couldn't get my mind to accept two such different things at the same time. On the one hand it was such a pretty scene, and at the very same time I could imagine, so clearly that it might have been real, that horrific night scene, with its group of uniformed police, with guns and with dogs, taking people away.

It was a very strange feeling, because I had been looking for Ignace for such a long time, and now I felt so close to him, as if I could just walk down the alley and knock on the door of number 12 and talk to him.

At first, for one shameful second, I had that familiar feeling of the excitement of discovery, of finally finding what you have been searching for, for so long. But this was very, very different. This time, finding what I had been looking for was heartbreaking.

Ignace was a person, a man who had had parents, who had wanted a better life. He lived not millions of years ago but only seventy years ago. Ignace could even have been a person in Mrs. E.'s family. Ignace had a younger brother, just like I do. And Ignace was murdered in the most horrible way imaginable.

I thought about my list of 're' words. *Remember, reveal, reclaim.* And then I thought of my new list: the 'pro' words. *Protect and protest.* If I was hoping to protect my fossils, and my ideas, and Jasper, and the memory of Ignace, it was not enough to find out the information and to write it in my notebooks. Ignace did not need me to be cataloguing the facts of his life and death in the way I catalogue my fossils. He did not need me to collect the information about his life and to keep it safe in a private notebook which only I would ever read, safe in my room.

You can't really protect anything without protesting against its being destroyed or lost. And you can't protest if you remain silent.

I took one step into the alleyway and stopped there because I was having a minor Heart Attacker. This is where the police had come into the alleyway, and at the other end, in the shadow, I could see how the passage was blocked, so even if you wanted to run you couldn't get away through the other end. This was where he lived and just there he would have bought his croissant every morning on his way to work and here was the front door of his flat where the police had stood with their guns, and here he was led away at gunpoint by the French police, and taken to Drancy.

28

The secret knowledge of things

I wrote this paper for my English teacher even though the school year was over and I was moving up a class and I would have a whole new bunch of teachers. But it felt like I hadn't really finished the story, so I sent her this paper in the post, even though I didn't need to do it and I wasn't ever going to get any marks or credit for it.

Searching for Ignace Edelstein (Part 3)

By Amethyst Simons

This is what I think it was like for Ignace Edelstein, in the days before he was arrested by the French police for being a Jew.

He and Andre lived in a small, narrow passageway between two rows of rather grand buildings. Even though their flat was small, and rather dark, it was in a very good area, near the centre of town.

Their flat was, for Ignace, in the perfect place: central, around the corner from a bakery where they bought their daily baguettes or croissants on the way to work. And nearby, in the same area, were other artists, and other jewellers and designers, leading the way in Parisian design. It was what he had dreamed of, and it was for this that he had left Turkey and moved to Paris.

Perhaps he worked for a firm which manufactured jewellery for the famous jewellery house, Bernard Herz. Herz was an important dealer in stones and pearls in Paris, and his company was known all over Europe.

One of the top designers of that time, Suzanne Belperron, who even designed some jewellery for royalty, and whose work to this day is in museum collections and is sold on auctions and is worth a fortune, worked with the Herz jewellery house. Her designs were new and different; she broke away from the style of jewellery of the time. She tried using different materials: instead of making jewellery in the usual way, setting precious stones in metal, she used stones, crystals and quartz, as settings, and then inlaid precious stones into the carved stone.

Stone into stone.

And that is why Ignace loved his work so much: he could work with stone, shape it, and make it look like it was soft and curved instead of hard and angular. He could polish it to make it shine like metal or finish it so it looked matte or rough.

Perhaps he became known at the Herz house as the maker who could carry out her new designs, who could see her vision. Perhaps they were a good team, he and Suzanne Belperron.

Ignace loved his work and he was good at it. He was surrounded by other jewellers, working in a large, brightly-lit workshop. He worked quietly, slowly and carefully; his work was precise and accurate, and he became known for the perfection of his creations.

Every day there were new designs, and the technicians had to invent new techniques to achieve the look the designers wanted. They were working with precious metals and exquisite precious stones, and there was a feeling of excitement because they were searching and learning and finding new ways to do things, but at the same time working with absolute accuracy so as not to damage the stones in any way.

Then the war started. Germany invaded France in May 1940. Paris was taken, or maybe gave up the fight, on June 14th 1940. By 1941 all of France was suffering: there were food shortages and fuel shortages. The German army requisitioned anything they could use for their building projects and for their war.

There were new laws all the time, affecting mostly Jews. Jews were not allowed to own businesses or work in certain jobs. Jews were not allowed to change their address. They had to sit in the last carriage on the Metro. Jewish shop windows were being marked out. Synagogues were vandalized and destroyed. Jews were not allowed to have a phone in their house, or to use a public phone.

On the 20th of August, 1941, the French police raided Jewish homes in the 11th District of Paris, not far from where Ignace and Andre lived, and arrested more than four thousand Jews. Most of them were foreign, not French-born Jews. They were the first to be sent to Drancy.

Nobody knew what would become of the people arrested, if or when they might be released.

Rumours were flying. Jews were not allowed to meet in public places like parks and theatres and cafes. Some people left Paris and tried to escape to the South, and a few of Ignace's friends tried to go back to Turkey, but they were turned back at the border because they had no papers or the wrong papers.

Ignace and Andre stayed on in their flat. Ignace carried on working, in spite of the growing feelings of fear and despair.

Andre had been working late recently. Ignace was worried: Andre had become secretive, going out at odd times and coming back late. Whenever Ignace asked him where he had been, all he would say was "Better you don't ask."

Ignace was sure Andre was getting involved in the Resistance, especially after August 1941 when Jews were forbidden from keeping radios in their houses. Andre was a radio technician; he had not one but three radios. One night, after it was announced that all radios owned by Jews would be confiscated, he packed the radios into large bags and disappeared, in spite of the curfew which forbade Jews to be out on the streets at night. He came back five hours later with his eyes wild and his hair on end but he said nothing to Ignace, refused to say where he had been and went to bed without saying a word.

When Ignace came home from work that evening in July, he was not surprised that Andre was not home; lately his brother was out more than he was at home.

Ignace made himself a sandwich because he was too tired and too worried to make dinner. He was sitting and eating when suddenly there was a very loud banging on the door and a shouted command.

"Open up! Police!"

Ignace was not stupid and he was not blind. He knew what was happening in Paris; he knew that twice already Jews had been rounded up by the French police. Jewish lawyers, doctors and scientists had been a special target and were arrested and sent to the detention centre in Drancy. Many of the first people arrested were foreign Jews, not Jews born in France. He was one of those, a foreigner, born in Turkey, a probable target. But nobody believes it can happen to them.

Useless to try to run; the street was crowded with police and dogs. There was no back door to his apartment. No time to think; they were banging on the door, banging and shouting.

If he could at least warn Andre. Ignace was terrified that Andre might come home at any minute and get caught.

He and Andre had an agreement, a secret code, which Andre had insisted on when the arrests first started. Ignace had initially been upset when Andre suggested it, because it had made him even more convinced that Andre was in the Resistance, but Andre had insisted and Ignace had agreed.

The code was that if either of them, coming home, saw that on the windowsill of their front window, the one facing the alley, was their mother's old brass coffee pot, which Ignace had brought with him from Turkey in a moment of sentimentality, it was a sign of danger, a sign to stay away and not to come near the house.

So the last thing Ignace did before opening the door to the police was to put the coffee pot on the windowsill.

As he was marched to the police van he saw his neighbours watching him. They said nothing, they didn't protest, they didn't ask him where he was going, and they turned their gaze away so that they didn't meet his eye.

The next morning, nothing had changed in Impasse Briare. People bought their croissants as usual, and went to work.

You may wonder how it is that I started to feel that I knew something more about Ignace than just the dates and places and the history I had been reading about the Holocaust. What I mean is, I got to know more than just the facts about the Jews who had been deported; I got to know *him*.

Something similar happened a long time ago when I was going to Mrs. E. for speech therapy. I must have been five years old and I had not been going to her for very long. I had been playing for a few weeks with the same things, because I couldn't speak and tell her I wanted something new to play with. I knew there were lots of toys in the cupboard because she had shown me, but I couldn't ask her, and I certainly couldn't walk over to the cupboard because then she would have looked at me and wondered what I was doing, and maybe she would have asked me and expected me to answer. I didn't know how to ask her, or what to say, and each time I thought about it my heart started to beat too fast, so I just kept quiet.

But there was always something strange about Mrs. E. and I really think she can read people's minds. I know this is not something most people would believe. I looked it up and I have made a list of a few of the words which mean something similar: *extra-sensory perception, mindreading, parapsychology, intuition*. Also, something I found when I was reading about speech therapy, '*theory of mind.*' This means that you are aware that other people can have thoughts which are different from your own thoughts and ideas. I read that some people don't have this ability at all; these people just can't imagine what other people may be thinking.

I think perhaps Mrs. E. is gifted in that way, in the same way that my brother Jasper is gifted at maths and magic tricks. Perhaps there isn't really anything magical at all in what she does; perhaps that is something that some good teachers just know how to do. But still I don't know how she does it, because one day when I was thinking about those other toys in the cupboard, she suddenly said, "I wonder if we could look at some different toys today," and she opened the cupboard and took out a new game.

So somehow she got to know me as a person: she knew what I needed at the time, even though I had not yet said a single word to her. Not one.

There were a few other times when that happened with Mrs. E., when she seemed to read my mind. I told you about that memory game, where you have pairs of identical cards. You put them facing down, all mixed up, and by turning over two cards, one at a time, you have try to find both cards of the pair, and the person who has the most pairs in the end is the winner.

When I first went to see her, I liked playing the memory game because I didn't have to talk at all to play the game. That was before I made progress and she wanted me to say the name of the picture I had picked up. In those early sessions when I was still not talking to her at all, all I had to do was find another picture, but she would sometimes talk; she would say things like "Hmm, I wonder where I saw the picture of that peacock, I know we saw it somewhere!" and what she was saying was exactly what I was thinking when I was searching for a specific picture. So you can see what I mean when I say I thought she could read minds.

Of course, now I know that what she said then is what anyone playing that kind of game would be thinking. You don't have to be a mind reader to know that. And now I know that she was doing that to help me feel that she and I could communicate, even if I had no words at all. But still, it somehow made me feel good to know that I didn't have to speak, and that she could somehow speak for me and say aloud exactly what I was thinking at exactly that moment. It was like a silent message passing between us.

And I think something like that happened with me when I was searching for Ignace.

29

The quality of perfection

The papers I wrote for my English teacher, about Ignace, are based on the few true facts that I found out in my research. The facts were a few dates and a few places, and a profession. I knew so little about him. But gradually, through all the months when I was searching for him, I was applying the strategies of the search: starting from what I knew, looking for clues. Getting my eye in, setting up a hypothesis, using small steps. I was tracking, I was creating a story, and trying to see into his mind, so that I could build up a picture of a person.

Some of what I have written is true and is based on research: what it was like in Turkey at that time, how young people were moving to Paris, the Paris exhibition in 1937, and what Paris was like during the German occupation. What it was like in Drancy, the address where Ignace and Andre lived, and their professions: all facts.

I don't know for sure if Ignace worked for the Herz jewellery company, but it is true that Bernard Herz really was a famous dealer in stones and pearls in Paris, and Suzanne Belperron really was the leading jewellery designer of the time who joined Herz and was allowed to design anything she wanted for Maison Bernard Herz. And it is true that some of her designs involved setting precious stones into stone instead of metal, which of course was something which excited me because of my ideas about xenoliths.

Bernard Herz, the wealthy and famous jeweller, came to the same end as Ignace. His name is also listed on the granite memorial wall in Paris. These are the few details we have about him: born on 31st May 1877, deported on convoy number 59 from Drancy to Auschwitz on the 2nd of September 1943. He died there in the same year.

Of his convoy of 1000 people, only 13 men survived, and Bernard Herz was not one of them. Perhaps because he was 66 when he arrived in Auschwitz; the Nazis would have considered him too old to be useful as a labourer.

Mrs. E. is 63; my grandmother is 68. Both of them would have been considered too old to deserve to live.

Suzanne Belperron was not a Jew but she was arrested for being in partnership with Bernard Herz. It was forbidden to operate a business with a Jew, or to run a business under a Jewish name. So for a while they ran the business under her name, but after she was arrested, the teamwork of Suzanne Belperron and Bernard Herz came to an end.

Suzanne, unlike Ignace and Bernard Herz, was released from prison, and she went on to work in the Resistance, and to run the business and to save it for Bernard's son Jean who survived the camps and came back to Paris and to his work after the war.

Those are the facts. So you may be thinking that everything else I have written here is invented, or imagined, and only a hypothesis, but it may also be that I have found the real Ignace.

I wonder what he would have thought of me, searching for his life like a detective, trying to keep something of him alive even though he was murdered so long ago and even though I don't know of any person in the whole world who was related to him or who knew him or his family. Maybe he would have thought, like many other people think, that I am weird. As strange as a xenolith: different from the other people around me, somehow caught in a group of people where I don't really belong. Spending all my free time, as well as my homework time, searching for a dead person.

But I think that in some ways I am like Ignace, and he is like me.

Our fascination with stones, for a start. I can imagine him sorting through the polished gemstones at his work, carefully catalogued and kept in a box just like my tool boxes, with little compartments, to find the right stone for a particular design he was working on.

I can imagine him spending hours with little notebooks, drawing the brooches or rings he was going to make, working out how to construct them.

I share with him his perfectionism, which is something my parents think is a failing in me, but which meant he would spend hours at work, cutting, polishing, working and reworking each piece until it was perfect. The perfectionism which made him such a talented jeweller, which might have allowed him to work on the designs of Belperron, to make her inventive and unusual designs work as a piece of jewellery which someone could wear. To find new techniques to make stone look like metal, to fit stones into stones, to create a xenolith.

The most beautiful xenoliths you can imagine.

I can imagine how carefully he needed to look at each piece, to choose just the right crystal which would give the perfect texture, or to choose the diamond with the greatest clarity and the best colour. I can see him looking carefully, slowly, peering through his special jeweller's magnifying loupe, at each facet, getting his eye in, just like I do when I am examining my fossils. I use a magnifying lens too, when I want to look more closely at the tiny details of a fossil or a stone which you can't see with the naked eye.

That kind of looking is not something everybody knows how to do.

Ignace and I have another thing in common: we feel a kind of responsibility to our younger brothers, even though those brothers don't want to be looked after and are sometimes just irritating to be around.

I can also imagine that he might have been a bit more quiet than his outgoing younger brother; he might have spent his evenings after long days at work, just drawing and planning and designing at home in his apartment in Impasse Briare, while his brother Andre was out with friends. Or while Andre was talking on his beloved radios, talking to the whole world, as if just talking with the person in the room with you is not enough.

I think Ignace was a person who might have understood how someone can be a bit different, can have a *Strategy of Perfection* and a *Strategy of Small Steps*, and even a *Strategy of Silence*.

Maybe we wouldn't have said a word to each other if we had met. We wouldn't have needed to, because he and I are so alike. We would sit and do our work, he would be choosing a stone and planning how to construct the piece of jewellery he was working on, and I would be sorting and labelling my fossils, with the place and date on which I found them, or entering new words in my dictionary, and we would be busy with our strategies, sitting silently but not alone.

Or maybe we would have talked. I know I said that I don't like small talk, and I don't chat. But maybe we would have talked about how he tried to save his brother, and whether I would have been brave enough to save Jasper if I had been in that situation.

Ignace: Amethyst. Is that you? We finally meet. I read your story, about how you searched for me. I was astonished how much you found out about me.

Amethyst: Well, if not for the internet I probably wouldn't have found anything.

Ignace: In that case maybe it is just as well that it took seventy years before someone thought of trying to find me, because in the meantime the internet was invented. But it hasn't been easy for me to wait, all these years, hoping someone would come and search for me.

Amethyst: What was amazing for me was to find that you were a jeweller, and that your surname means gemstone. Because my name is the name of a stone too.

Ignace: Well, what is amazing to me is how you persevered, how many hours you spent searching for me. I don't think I was half as scientific as you when I was your age, and I definitely didn't have half the perseverance you have.

Amethyst: I hope you don't think it was cheeky to make up those things about you, all the things I wrote about why you left Turkey and the secret code you had with your brother. It's just that I found so few facts about you, and I needed to be able to imagine you as a real person before I could become a proper guardian for you.

Ignace: Well, you got very close to the real me. But I have something to say. It is about participation. I read all that stuff you wrote about the teachers who wanted you to participate more, to be part of a team. But the way I see it, you worked so hard searching for me, you spent so much time participating in my life, that if anyone is a real participator, it is you. What I want you to know is that a participator is not always the person who talks. It is the person who actually does things, who takes on a job like you did, who does the work. Researching, recovering, retrieving.

Amethyst: Well I hope that is what I will do when I leave school. I want to be a palaeontologist or a detective. But now, the thing is, now that I have found you, and I have written your story, I don't know what to do next. You have been such a big part of what I did every day, for months and months.

Ignace: Well, you have got to know me, but I have read what you wrote, so I have also got to know you, and your family, and even Mrs. E. So I wonder: what would Mrs. E. say?

Amethyst: She would probably say "I wonder…" and then she would say that she doesn't know the answer, she needs to think a while, and can we discuss it next week.

30

The strategies of silence

I wrote this paper for myself, not for any teacher. I wrote it in the Moleskine notebook where I keep all the information I found about Ignace.

I wrote it without thinking too much, without planning or setting out the main ideas, as my English teacher would have preferred; it sort of poured out of me in one go. I think in a way it helped me to face up to the sadness, the loss, I was feeling at having found Ignace in one way but in another way knowing, at the very same time, that he could never be found, and that only his name remains.

The Strategies of Silence

By Amethyst Simons

When I was five I didn't speak at school for a whole year.

Now I am thirteen and I speak when I want to, but I often choose not to speak: to children who irritate me, and to certain adults. Silence is for me a choice and a preference. You could call it 'a strategy of silence.'

I sometimes choose silence as a way to keep my thoughts, my ideas, pure and untouched. If I have to argue with people who don't like the way I am, who don't like my ideas, I feel my ideas get spoiled; they get diluted.

There are lots of reasons for choosing silence. What is said cannot be unsaid. I know that some kids say I am weird, and that hurts. If you say something stupid or something hurtful to someone else, it has a kind of permanence to it, like words engraved in granite, which can last for thousands of years. Like the hieroglyphs on Cleopatra's Needle.

Sometimes silence is simply the appropriate thing, the right thing to do at the time. If you are ever in a bird hide, watching through the narrow window slits, trying to see what is going on out there in the bird world, you will know how to be silent and to guard that silence. Nobody talks above a whisper in a hide. That space is not ours, it belongs to the birds and we can stay there only if we can keep silent.

There is another thing I want to say about silence. If you are talking to someone, you have to be really silent so that you can listen to what they are saying.

I know this from watching what happens in classroom discussions. People think I am not participating but I am actually listening and observing. I get my eye in and I look very carefully, and I see things. And what I see is that very often, people don't really listen to anyone else; they are using the time while someone else is talking to prepare their case so that they can say again exactly what they said before.

By not listening, they don't hear any new ideas.

To have a proper discussion, which is supposed to be a dialogue, you have to stop thinking about your own ideas and listen to the other person, and then the other person has to stop thinking about his own ideas and be silent while he waits to hear what someone else is saying.

Dialogue: from the Greek words 'dio' meaning two, and 'logos' meaning speech.

So in a discussion, silence is not the problem. In a discussion, silence can be the solution.

And that is why I don't like to take part in discussions in class; because I know a lot about silence and I think very few people know how to be silent.

My grandmother does know about silence; and so does my homework coach, Mrs. E. She is often silent for a long time. I sometimes wonder if people would think she is doing her job, if they would see us, just sitting silently together, but she is one of the few people who knows how to really be silent and to listen, and who doesn't think silence is a problem.

Silence as a choice has been used in spiritual activity for ages. The Quakers use silence in their prayer services; people all over the world are learning to meditate and to try to silence the noise in their minds.

But my silence is not a spiritual quest. I think part of my silence these days may be because I am sometimes not sure what the right thing is to say, especially if there are lots of people listening, like in class, or at parties, which I don't often go to. I feel clumsy; I feel awkward. I have to choose what to say and in the end I often say nothing. I once heard someone say something about 'the embarrassment of being alive', and I understand what that means.

My silence didn't feel like a choice when I was five. It was a phobia. At least that is how selective mutism is seen these days by speech therapists, who are the people most likely to be asked to help someone like me.

The problem about being a person who is often silent is that it can become a habit. It may start off as your armour, your protection, but after a few years you feel that it is not armour but rather a part of you. At that stage you are used to having your own thoughts, used to working through problems on your own, used to not needing to talk things through with other people.

That may be a good thing – it may make you an independent thinker; but it may be a bad thing because it can make you anti-social and irritate your teachers. And it can prevent you from discussing things with someone who might say something useful for you to think about.

To be honest, I am not even sure if my silence is entirely a choice these days, now that I am thirteen. Because I do know how to talk, and I do participate in class these days, a little anyway, just enough to keep the teachers off my back. But my silence is perhaps just because of who I am. I am different from other people and that is not a problem for me, though it may be a problem for my teachers.

But even if you know your preference for silence may not be a totally positive thing when taken to extremes, it is something that exists. You become an observer, a watcher. You become more competent at watching people and picking up clues to their feelings. You can read the momentary shifts of facial expression which most people can't even see; you can see into a person's mind and you can get to know a person even if no words have been exchanged. Maybe you get to know things about people that they would prefer nobody to know; maybe you know things about them that they don't even know about themselves.

And when you need to break out of that silence, you feel the awkwardness of it, and you feel stuck.

For a long time, when I was seeing Mrs. E., I thought about silence as a preference, or as a strategy. But there is a different kind of silence: the silence of death.

If you are murdered you have no choice about whether to be silent or not. After you are dead there are no choices at all. Ignace Edelstein is silent because he was murdered. He spoke until the age of 39 and then he was silenced.

I learned a lot about silence while I was searching for Ignace.

One of the things I learned about silence in my search for Ignace is that sometimes the only right thing to do is to be silent, because there is nothing that words can say that are right for some situations. When I try to find the words to talk about Ignace, and the seventy thousand Jewish people from France and the six million Jewish people from all over Europe, and all the Gypsies and disabled people and gay people who were murdered, words fail me and all I can find is silence. At first, when I first decided to be the Guardian of the Memory of Ignace Edelstein, I felt that perhaps silence was what I owed to Ignace and his brother, a silence of respect, because no words could express this event. Choosing to be silent seemed the only right thing to do. In memorial ceremonies there is usually a minute's silence. But a minute's silence didn't seem nearly enough. How much silence, then, would be enough? An hour? A year?

Lots of people say to me, what is so interesting about fossils? You find them, maybe the search is fun or exciting, but then you put them in a box, and there they stay. Stones don't do anything, they don't speak, so what is the point?

Well for me, there is a point, because fossils speak to me in the same way that sand speaks to my dad. You have to know how to listen inside the silence.

I am like a xenolith: a stone which lives surrounded by a completely different kind of stone. I am different from other kids, I don't often fit in, and the voice of a xenolith isn't often heard. You have to look hard to see a xenolith, and you have to listen carefully to hear what a xenolith can tell you.

I may not be a good speaker but I am a good listener. I had to listen very hard, for more than eight months, to be able to hear Ignace, because his voice was silenced when he was murdered. And now that I can hear him, I am a proper Guardian of his Memory: I participate in his life and that is how he can be remembered.

Of course Ignace would not have wanted to be silenced. He would have wanted to tell people who he was and what he did. He would have wanted to show people his work and to tell them what he was doing, to tell them about why he was such a perfectionist and how much he loved living in Paris. And he would have wanted to tell his parents that he tried to save Andre.

Something happened to me while I was searching for Ignace. I found, along the way, that my preferences shifted. Something happened to my strategy of silence, and something inside me changed. I will try to explain, but it's not simple, and it's not straightforward.

Maybe I can explain by using an analogy. In nature, things change with time. Even in geology. The sand dunes in the desert don't stay the same; they shift with the wind. If you study rocks, you will know that there is a thing called a rock cycle: rocks are constantly changing, over time. They are weathered, they are heated and melted and compressed and mixed with other materials, and they are moved around the earth by volcanoes and earthquakes and continental drift.

So any rock you find, even if you can name it and describe its physical and chemical properties, is in the process of becoming something different.

If a rock can change, then so can a person.

In Bruce Chatwin's book he describes how the people sing to keep the land alive.

So this book is my way of speaking about Ignace, or rather, of giving him a chance to make his own voice heard.

THE END

Postscript

After I finished writing this book I went back to the Wiener library for one more visit, just in case I had missed something. I was trawling through the list, also painstakingly compiled by Serge Klarsfeld, of the names of every child who was deported from France by the Nazis. 11,400 in all.

It makes heartbreaking reading: whole families, sometimes five or six siblings, taken in one go, and sent to Auschwitz. I didn't really know what I was searching for, as I had found all I could about Ignace and Andre. So I decided to look at every single home address given for the 11,400 children on this list, in the hope that I might find someone who might have lived on the same street as the brothers.

And after a few hours, incredibly, I found something. I found the names of two teenage girls, Sarah and Dora Kempinski, who lived at the same address as Ignace and Andre: 12, Impasse Briare, 9th Arondissement, Paris.

When I saw the address which had become so familiar to me, I wanted to shout, to say something, but everyone else in the library was sitting so quietly, working so hard, that I made myself stay quiet.

Sarah was born on 15th February 1926, and sent to the detention camp Pithiviers at age 16. She was deported on convoy number 13 on the 31st of July 1942. Dora, two years younger, was born 29th May 1928, and was sent, also via Pithiviers, on convoy 20, on August 17th 1942, to Auschwitz.

I have not found their death certificates so I don't know if they survived Auschwitz or not. I have searched for the names of the parents of these two girls without success. I have no idea why the girls were living at the same address as Ignace and Andre; I now presume that Ignace and Andre might have rented a room from the Kempinski family. But what happened to the girls' parents? The only other people by that name, on the entire list of 75,721 people, lived in different towns, not in Paris.

So now I have something else to search for, after all.

References

Selective mutism and quiet or shy children:

Collins, Janet. *The Quiet Child*. Cassell, 1996

Franklin, Joseph. *You're Never Alone*. Grosvenor House Publishing Ltd., 2014

Johnson, M. and Wintgens, A. *The Selective Mutism Resource Manual*. Speechmark, 2001

Johnson, M. and Wintgens, A. *Can I tell you about Selective Mutism? A guide for friends, family and professionals*. Jessica Kingsley, 2012

McHolm, A.E., Cunningham, C.E. and Vanier, M.K. *Helping your Child with Selective Mutism*. New Harbinger Publications, 2006

Perednik, Ruth. *The Selective Mutism Treatment Guide*. Oaklands, 2011

Holocaust information sources:

Guardian of the Memory http://guardianofthememory. org/about [Accessed March 2015]

Josephs, J. *Swastika over Paris*. Bloomsbury, 1989

Klarsfeld, Serge and Beata http://klarsfeldfoundation.org/ [Accessed March 2015]

Neher, Andre. *The Exile of the Word: From the Silence of the Bible to the Silence of Auschwitz*. The Jewish Publication Society of America, 1981

Yad Vashem http://www.yadvashem.org/yv/en/about/index.asp [Accessed March 2015]

Other sources:

Angelou, Maya. *I Know Why the Caged Bird Sings*. Virago, 1984

Boynton, Sandra. *Fifteen Animals*. Workman Publishing Company Inc., New York, 2008

Celan, Paul. *Selected Poems*. Penguin Books, 1995

Chatwin Bruce. *The Songlines*. Vintage Classics, 1998

Fortey, Richard. *Trilobite! Eyewitness to Evolution*. Vintage Books, 2000

Liebenberg, Louis. *The Art of Tracking*. David Philip, 2001

Walker, C. and Ward, D. *Fossils*. Dorling Kindersley, 1992

Welland, M. *Sand: a Journey through Science and the Imagination*. Oxford University Press, 2009

White, Michael. *Maps of Narrative Practice*. Norton and Co., London, 2007

Lightning Source UK Ltd.
Milton Keynes UK
UKOW06f2113180615

253758UK00001B/1/P